10/

Di

Choi

Here you made a good choice!

Choices

edited by
Christopher C Teague

First Published in 2006 by
Pendragon Press
Po Box 12, Maesteg, Mid Glamorgan
South Wales, CF34 0XG, UK

Typesetting and design by
Christopher Teague

Printed in Wales by
MWL, Pontypool

ISBN-10: 0 9554452 0 5
ISBN-13: 978 0 9554452 0 0

Contents

Last Kiss

Andrew Humphrey

We were halfway around the Crome Gallery when Becky started crying again. I didn't notice at first. I was reading a poem by Andrew Motion that was printed on Perspex and mounted on the gallery wall. It was his tribute to the Norwich School of Artists. It was all right, I thought, what I understood of it.

Becky had her back to me as she studied a self-portrait by John Crome. I glanced at her casually. My first thought was that she still looked good in jeans. Then I saw that her head was trembling and that she held her right hand against her face.

"Becky," I said.

She raised her hand suddenly, fingers splayed. It was a little melodramatic, I thought. "I'm ok."

"You're obviously not." Mr Perceptive. I moved to her side, touched her waist, then, for some reason, her head. Her hair, although long, black and beautiful, was greasier than it looked. I let my hand drop, wiped my fingers surreptitiously on the bottom of my sweater. "How long have you been crying?"

"About six months." Her voice was small and stiff. A child's voice. It didn't sit well on a woman of forty. I stifled a sigh. "I can see your face in the reflection," she said.

So she could. I tried to look sympathetic, failed.

"People will see," I said.

"The place is empty, John." As though that, too, was my fault.

The trip to the art gallery in Norwich's Castle Museum was for her benefit. Becky had studied art years ago. In her twenties she produced a string of competent watercolours and held a joint exhibition with a friend in one of Norwich's smaller galleries. I never saw her work. She burnt them all a year before she met me. She started sketching again after the second miscarriage. There was a folder full of drawings in our bedroom; small, intense, bitter things that I couldn't bear to look at. They were good, but awful, if you know what I mean.

I barely knew an oil painting from a watercolour. I could think of better things to do on a Sunday afternoon. Liverpool versus Chelsea was on Sky for a start.

We drank coffee on a wooden bench outside the Castle's café as Becky's eyes dried. It was grey and cold. The low sky was stiff with cloud. A small but persistently frigid breeze reminded me why I hate January.

"We could go inside," I said. "A bit radical, I know, what with it being winter and all."

"I like it out here." Her nose and cheeks were red with cold. She hunched into her jacket.

"You're a strange little woman, aren't you?"

"Don't patronise me."

"And what would you have me do?" I lent forward, touched her nose with mine, kissed her mouth and waited for her to kiss me back. She did. She always did.

"I'm sorry I cried."

"No you're not," I said. "You just wanted some attention."

"Bastard," she said.

I shrugged. "By the way, I'm out tonight."

"With Charlie, I suppose."

"If the wind changes you'll stay like that."

"You know what I think of Charlie."

"Well, we're all bastards, aren't we?" She didn't smile. "You're welcome to join us. It's just a couple of drinks, nothing special."

"I don't think so."

"You'll stay in on your own. As usual."

"You could keep me company."

“I could. I’m not going to.”

She sulked for the rest of the afternoon. I ignored her. Which was why she loved me.

I met Charlie at the Walnut Tree Shades in the city centre.

“You’re late,” he said.

“As usual.”

“And yet I was still early. What does that say about me?”

“That you’re a pillock?”

He bought me a drink. We stood at the bar although there were tables free. Charlie dumped a whiskey into what was left of his lager. He drained the glass and smacked his lips. “That’s better,” he said. He was tallish, about my height, but slimmer, with dark hair that was long enough and just the right side of lank. He was sporting the beginnings of a goatee. It suited him but I wasn’t going to tell him that. The barmaid kept glancing at him. He didn’t even notice. Becky fancied him. Hated him but fancied him. Which was ok. I didn’t like him much but I enjoyed his company.

“I suppose Becky is languishing on her own.”

“Just to buck a trend.”

“What a waste.”

“Her choice.”

“I meant, her being married to you.”

“So did I.”

We drank quickly. I don’t know why. I’d told Becky the truth. It was meant to be a quiet night. It seemed Charlie had other ideas.

“I know somewhere we can go. When the pubs are shut.”

“A party?”

“Something like that.”

“On a Sunday night?”

He tapped the side of his nose. His eyes were beginning to glaze but he was steady enough on his feet and his speech was clear. “As I always say, it’s who you know.”

Charlie. By day humble insurance clerk, by night bass player in a Pink Floyd tribute band. Very rock and roll. He got invited to some good parties, though.

"But it's a Sunday night."

"You're getting old, John."

This was true. "You have work tomorrow?"

"Yep. Don't care. I'm hardcore."

"So I'm told. I've got a day off. Jealous?"

"A bit. And so you have no excuse."

"Dunno. I've still got to get up early." Charlie looked blank. "Becky thinks I'm going to work."

"You bastard."

"I just need a day on my own."

"On your own? Not planning a little trip to Cromer, then?"

I fixed my gaze onto the stamped tin ceiling. The pub was full now and the air was thick with cigarette smoke and mingled conversations. Something bluesy played in the background. "Don't know yet."

"That's bollocks."

"You should try living with Becky."

"Anytime."

I think he meant it. But as I'd told him many times before, words are easy.

I drank some more. So did Charlie.

"The thing is, you'll fuck it up. And then you'll regret it." His voice was softer, reflective.

"And you'd be there to pick up the pieces?"

"I know what she thinks of me."

"She'd fuck you, at a pinch."

"Well, who wouldn't?" he said. But something in his face changed.

"Ten years and counting, Charlie. She needs me."

"My point exactly."

"She needs me how I am."

He raised his eyebrows. "Really?"

"She's been indulged all her life. By her parents, by an army of therapists. By that useless wanker of a first husband. All pandering to poor little Becky."

Charlie looked uncomfortable. "But…"

"What? The miscarriages? Sad," I said. "But shit happens. And she was like this anyway. Self-indulgent. Depressive." I was angry and wasn't sure why. "It's just another excuse."

"Excuse? Do you realise how cold you sound?"

"Yes. I do. You know, she never wanted kids. Not really. And she would have been a crap mother."

"Jesus."

I'd drunk too much. That didn't make what I was saying any less true. "To be honest, when she told me…about the first one? I was relieved. I didn't want kids, either. Not with her."

"You bastard," Charlie said softly.

"That word again," I said.

All expression dropped from his face. He didn't look at me or speak to me for fifteen minutes.

Eventually I said, "Well, am I still invited to this party?"

"Fuck it, yeah," Charlie said. "I'm not going on my own."

It was a waste of time. We arrived at a large Victorian terrace house on the outskirts of Thorpe just after eleven to find a handful of men and precisely three women, all older than me, scattered throughout a number of cold, cavernous rooms. I didn't recognise the music, but it was awful. Some bastard soft-country-rock hybrid. There was little to drink and the buffet had long since been picked clean. The bright spark who'd invited Charlie wasn't even present.

"Hardcore," I said.

"It's not quite what I expected," Charlie said.

"You astonish me."

We lasted until midnight.

"Another taxi?" I said, as we stood on the front path, hunched into our jackets, breath billowing in the cold air.

"I think I'll walk," Charlie said.

"But it's miles. And it's freezing."

"I'm wide awake and as sober as a judge."

"Nothing like a crap party to sober you up."

"Precisely. And I fancy a walk."

"I suppose I'd better keep you company."

"I'm a big boy. I think I can manage."

"If something happened to you I'd never forgive myself."

"Right. That and you're too tight to pay for a taxi on your own."

"How well you know me."

We took a shortcut, through a field, past a disused children's playground, into a clearing that led to an old bridge that led across the railway tracks. I think I was teasing Charlie about his band as we approached the bridge. He had a couple of gigs later in the week.

"So what will you be playing? Don't tell me – Money. The Wall. Dark Side of the Moon. Just for a change."

"Funny man."

"Don't you get sick of it?"

"Most bands play the same stuff over and over." His voice was flat. I was getting to him.

"Yeah, but most bands aren't pretending to be somebody else. What's that all about?"

"Fuck you, John."

It was familiar ground. I suppose it irritated me, Charlie playing in a tribute band. He was a talented musician and I couldn't understand why he wasn't writing and performing his own material. He simply wasn't interested. Which I suppose was his business. Perhaps I was just jealous because he had a talent and I didn't.

Irritated, Charlie took the lead as we approached the steep metal steps that led to the bridge's walkway. He clattered up them briskly then stopped when he reached the top. I almost bumped into him.

"Wait," Charlie said.

I peered over his shoulder. "Shit," I said.

Halfway along the bridge, on the wrong side of the safety rail, stood on the narrow stone parapet was the figure of a man. He was silhouetted against the moonlight, slender and unmoving. His arms were angled out behind him, hands grasping the safety rail.

After a moment Charlie walked towards him. "You all right, mate?" His voice was bright and normal.

"Easy," I said as I scuttled up behind him.

"What are you up to?" Charlie said.

"What do you think?" the man said. His voice was conversational, amused. He was in his twenties, I supposed, with a smooth, cherubic face and thinning, sandy hair.

Charlie slapped me on the back. "You heard the man. Let's go."

"What?"

"I've got work tomorrow. I don't want to fuck about."

"You can't be serious."

Charlie glanced at the man, who gazed into the distance, his face expressionless. "This is none of our business." I just looked at him. He shrugged. "It's not even that much of a drop."

I peered over the edge of the parapet. It looked far enough to me. The railway tracks, cut deep into the embankment, seemed a long way below.

"Perhaps he'll just break a leg or something," Charlie said. "Or he could end up a vegetable. If he takes my advice, he'll trot into the city centre. Try the car park at St Stephens. It's a dead cert. If you'll excuse the expression."

"Thanks," the man said. "But I think this will do."

"Your funeral," Charlie said.

"What the hell is the matter with you?" I said.

"What?" he said, all innocence, arms open wide. "I'm off. You coming?"

"No," I said.

His arms dropped slowly to his sides. "Found your conscience, John?"

"I've always had a conscience," I said quickly. Perhaps a little too quickly.

"Do you think Becky would agree?"

He held a half smile as I looked at him. "This is different."

"Sure. You don't even know this guy." I started to say something else but Charlie turned and flung an arm up and said, "I'm gone. You do what you want."

I watched as he walked into the darkness.

"You can go too," the man said. I turned back towards him. His head was twisted in my direction. He wore only a thin sweater and a pair of jeans but if he was cold he didn't show it. "No-one will know. Your friend is right. This is nothing to do with you. It's not your fault."

"I can't just walk away."

"Actually, you can." The truth is I wanted to. I was cold and tired. He gave a thin smile. "And it might get messy."

But some of Charlie's comments had struck a nerve. "What's your name?"

"Luke. Not that it matters."

"I'm John."

"Well, that's two of the Disciples sorted."

There was a silence. It dragged on. I didn't have a clue what to say next. Luke was calm and still. He didn't appear to be in a hurry. I don't think I ever believed he would actually jump. Not while I was there.

Belatedly I remembered my mobile. I pulled it out of my jacket, flicked it open.

"Don't," Luke said mildly. "If you make a call, I'll jump."

I put the phone away. "There's no-one you want to contact?"

"No."

I moved closer to the rail. "Why are you doing this?"

"That's my business."

"It's just…you seem so calm."

"Why wouldn't I be? I'm in control for once."

"Is that what this is about? Control?"

Luke sighed. "I know you mean well, John, but please, spare me the cod psychology."

I felt my cheeks flush. I was glad he wasn't looking at me. "Sorry," I said.

"No problem."

I shifted position. My feet ached. I wondered if anyone else would come past. I hoped that they would. Someone who knew what they were doing.

"Have you been here long?" I said.

"Long enough. Hours, I suppose. But that's nothing, is it? Not in the scheme of things."

"And no-one else has tried to help?"

"Nope. Just you. Aren't you special." His voice was flat and colourless and although it sounded as though he was taking the piss it was hard to be sure.

"I'm surprised, that's all."

Luke grunted.

And I thought maybe Charlie had been right. He'd be halfway home by now. I was being mocked by somebody I'd never met before. If he jumped it would be…unpleasant. Inconvenient. But would I actually care? No. Of course I wouldn't. But at least I had tried to help. That was something. Wasn't it?

"You're right," Luke said.

"What?"

"Just fuck off. I'll be fine." His voice had changed. It was lower, gruffer.

"What are you talking about?"

"I didn't ask for an audience."

I nearly left. I wish now that I had. "Well, you've got one. And how come you've been here hours? What's that all about?"

"You think I'm having second thoughts?"

"Yep. Don't blame you. Lets face it, it's going to hurt, isn't it?"

"Fuck you," he said. He took his hands off the safety rail, leant forward a fraction.

"You selfish bastard," I said.

And he jumped. Actually, he didn't. But in my mind he did, and with such clarity that for a moment I thought it was real. In my mind he didn't jump as much as lean forward and let gravity take over. I heard the soft, muffled thump of his body hitting the tracks. I moved forward, intending to peer over the edge of the bridge, in order to satisfy a morbid curiosity.

In reality Luke still stood on the ledge, tensed slightly, eyes closed. Then he leant back and his hands found the safety rail again.

"Have I struck a chord?" I said.

After a moment he nodded.

"So there is someone?"

He said nothing. He stood for a while, without moving at all, as condensation formed on the metal bridge and the cold settled and deepened around us.

Finally I was about to speak, just to break the silence and the stillness of the night when Luke turned to me and said, "So, what do you do, John?"

As though we'd just met in a pub and I'd bought him a drink.

"What?"

"You're right. I'm selfish. It's all me, me, me. Tell me about yourself."

His voice seemed easy, more relaxed than it had been since I'd stumbled across him. But there was something behind it, a tension that also showed in his eyes as they met mine.

"I'm in IT. How boring is that?"

"But the money's good."

"Too good, really. For what I do, what I know. Money for old rope. Not that I'm complaining."

"And Becky?"

"Becky?"

"Your friend mentioned her. Your wife, I assume. What does she do?"

"Why?"

"Just making conversation. Humour me."

"She does nothing. Sometimes she stack shelves at Sainsbury's."

"Why say it like that? As though you're ashamed? Are you a snob, John?"

He turned as he spoke so that he had his back to the drop. He leant his elbows on the safety rail and stared at me. Full on, his features were wide and bland. And he looked older, I thought, than my initial impressions.

"No. I'm not clever enough to be a snob. I'm a lager and football man, me. Becky's got the brains, the education. But it's me that's on 25k. It annoys me, that's all."

"No children, then?"

"Is it that obvious?"

"From what you've just said, yes."

I shrugged and didn't speak.

"Am I being intrusive?" he said.

"A little."

"I'm sorry."

He levered himself over the safety rail and clambered onto the bridge. He walked up to me so that we were face to face, inches apart. I caught a hint of cologne. Something old-fashioned, that maybe my father would have worn.

Sandalwood, perhaps. I was taller and heavier than he was but, for no reason that I can think of, I felt physically threatened. I took a half step backwards.

"Will you make a call for me?" he said.

I grabbed my phone, handed it to him. "Help yourself."

He held up his hands. They were red and swollen from grasping the safety rail. "I don't think I could manage at the moment."

I nodded as I turned the phone on. "No signal," I said.

"Let's get off the bridge. Lead on," he said. He laid a hand on my shoulder and I hurried forward so that he was no longer touching me.

When I reached the far bank I checked my phone again.

"It's fine now," I said, turning. But Luke had gone.

When I got home I took a long shower and went to bed. Becky was there already, fully dressed, huddled beneath the covers, asleep. I pressed against her for warmth. She didn't stir. After a moment I realised that she smelled and I moved so that my back was to her. Becky can go days without changing her clothes and sometimes she forgets to wash herself or brush her teeth. In contrast to her personal hygiene she kept the house almost pathologically clean. And before she could leave a room every piece of furniture, every ornament had to be in exactly the right place. It drove me nuts sometimes.

It was a long while before I slept. The events on the bridge already seemed distant, unreal. I knew that in the morning I would doubt that they had actually happened at all.

But when I finally slept I dreamt of Luke. I saw him fall; from a bridge, a car park, from the top of the office where I work. His body tumbling through cold air. I saw him broken on concrete and stone, smeared across a live rail. His bland face, backlit, loomed above mine. For a brief, terrifying moment when I woke I was certain that Luke was beside me, twisted, wrecked, the bedclothes heavy and sodden with his blood. Then Becky belched quietly and stirred and the smell of her drifted over me. I lay on my back and felt my heart hammering in my chest.

I was out of the house by seven-thirty. Becky was asleep. When she was taking her medication she could sleep twelve hours a day, barely moving, and still need a nap in the afternoon.

It well before nine when I reached Cromer, too early to visit Helen. I parked in the town centre and found a café, where I took my time over a full English and a mug of weak coffee. I read the Eastern Daily Press from cover to cover. Riveting. The place was filling up and the waitress was shooting me dirty looks when I finally left.

The mist had thickened into fog. I tensed myself against the cold but the air was milder than it looked. Helen lived in a terraced house in a side road, parallel to the sea front. It took me fifteen minutes to reach it.

We'd had an affair five years earlier, Helen and I, when she'd briefly temped in my office. Our fling burnt itself out quickly but we kept in touch and slept together every now and then.

She answered the door in a cream towelling dressing gown that I remembered well. Her blond hair was tousled and she wore no make up. She looked great, though.

"I was hoping you still had Monday's off."

"It's been nine months."

I was surprised. I didn't think it was as long as that, but I did the math quickly and she was right. "I suppose it has."

"I didn't think…" She ran a hand through her hair. "You should have called."

I shrugged. She didn't move. "I'm cold," I lied.

"Tell me something I don't know," she said.

"What?"

"You'd better come in."

I followed her through the hallway. "You've redecorated," I said. "Terracotta. Nice."

"I'm glad you approve."

In the kitchen she lit a cigarette and made us coffee. I watched her from the table, as I'd done many times before.

"Nine months," I said. "I didn't realise."

"Time just rushes by when you're having fun, doesn't it?"

"I meant to keep in touch."

"A Christmas card would have been nice."

"You didn't send me one."

"It's a bit tricky, what with you being married."

I nodded. The kettle boiled. Helen stood for a moment, staring into the steam. There were tiny purple flowers embroidered along the hem of the dressing gown. I'd counted them once, while she fellated me.

"What is it?" I said.

"My dad died."

"I'm sorry."

"You never even met him."

"Still…"

"Heart attack. Last October. Two days before my birthday."

I didn't say anything. She made our coffee, dumped the spoon in the sink with a clatter and sat heavily opposite me.

"I nearly called you then."

"You should have."

She looked into my face. Her smile was so bleak I had to look away. "You'd have expected a fuck."

"Might have done you good," I said. I closed my eyes. "Shit. I'm sorry…"

She stood carefully and retrieved an ashtray from the worktop. "That was low, John. Even for you."

"I know. I'm sorry. It's just…Becky…"

She sat again, blew smoke angrily past my shoulder. "Spare me, please. I tell you my dad died and you want to have a bleat about the Basket Case."

I was quiet for a moment. "I think that's fifteen-all, don't you?"

She stubbed out her cigarette in three precise movements. "I'm seeing someone."

This wasn't unusual. The expression on her face was.

"So?"

"It's serious."

"And?"

She pushed the ashtray to one side and blew on her coffee. "I mean, moving in serious. Getting engaged serious. Not fucking around serious."

Even I knew that I had no right to feel hurt. But I did. And stupid and betrayed. But mostly hurt.

"Where did you meet this prince?"

"At a support group."

"A support group?"

"After dad died. His name's Dominic."

"Dominic? Jesus."

"Don't sneer, John."

"But it's my default setting. I thought you knew that."

She got up from the table and went to the sink where she stood with her back to me, her shoulders stiff and hunched. Hair colour aside, she could have been Becky; tallish, willowy, slender waist. For a moment I thought she was crying, but I was wrong. Because she wasn't Becky. Not at all. Which was most of the attraction. I think.

"Why are you here?" she said.

It was a good question but that didn't mean I had to answer it. Not honestly, at least.

"I would have thought it was obvious. Just the usual, that's all."

She turned and leant her back against the edge of the sink. Her arms were angled behind her, hands gripping the worktop. For a moment I thought of Luke. I looked at Helen's breasts, pushed upwards by the position of her shoulders, and shoved the thought aside.

"Really?" she said.

I adjusted my line of vision so that I met her eyes. "What else?" I stood. "I mean, you just caught me checking out your tits. That's me, isn't it? Typical bloke. Led by my dick."

"You sound angry, John."

"Angry? Really?" Actually I was almost shouting. I don't know why.

"I'm going to take a shower, get dressed. If you're still here we can walk into town, get a late breakfast."

"I've already eaten."

"Ok. Some more coffee, then."

"Are you going to counsel me?"

She was by the door now. She sighed. "You can wait here for me or you can fuck off. I'm not too fussed either way."

I waited.

When she came down again she wore grey tracksuit bottoms and a shapeless beige sweater that was too big for her. She shrugged an old anorak over her shoulders to complete the ensemble. I assume she was trying to make herself as unattractive as possible, trying to make things easier for me. It didn't work.

We walked down some concrete steps onto the beach and made our way towards the town. The fog had lifted a little. The sea was vast and still and gormless and the air smelled of brine, which was understandable under the circumstances. The beach was as empty as you'd expect it to be on a Monday morning in late January.

"We've been here before," I said.

"Are you speaking metaphorically?" Helen said.

"You'll just confuse me, using big words like that."

A gull screamed nearby and we both turned towards the sound.

"How rude," I said.

Helen tucked a stray hair behind an ear. She kept herself a couple of paces away from me. We *had* been here before and she knew it. The previous spring. It had been hot and we'd walked hand in hand, barely speaking. Thinking about it that was probably the last time I'd seen her.

"I don't think you're just after a shag," Helen said.

We paused for a moment, turned towards the sea.

"Wouldn't be the first time," I said. "After all, I *am* that shallow."

"Well, we agree on that." She tipped her head towards me, offered me a ghost of a smile.

"So?" I said.

She played with her hair again. She did that a lot. "You're different, that's all. Somehow." I waited. She shrugged. "I don't know. You're…sadder."

"Sadder?"

"Yeah. Something like that. Beneath all the bullshit."

She was right, but I wasn't going to admit it. It was Becky, I suppose. Living with her wasn't getting any easier, wasn't likely to in the foreseeable future. I don't know what I expected Helen to do about it. We just screwed each other now and then. It wasn't as though I loved her or anything.

But I found it hard to look at her.

When we got to the town we got coffee to go and sat on a wooden bench next to an ice-cream parlour and looked out at the sea. Helen told me a little about Dominic and I nodded in the right places and tried to look interested. She was happy and I should have been glad and of course I wasn't. I'd wanted her to be miserable, alone, glad to see me. What exactly we could have done for each other I don't know. I hadn't looked that far ahead. I never do.

I asked some questions, forced a brightness into my voice that was entirely false. I realised I was dragging it out. Once she was gone that was it. We'd never been friends, exactly. We had nothing in common except an occasional mutual desire. Which now wasn't mutual any more. And I'd been kidding myself that what I felt was something more than simple desire.

No fool like an old fool. Except that I'm not that old.

I stood and tossed my empty cardboard cup into the bin that was by the bench. Helen stood as well. She was halfway through a sentence and I waited for her to go on but she didn't.

"Good luck with the whole Dominic thing," I said.

She nodded and shivered a little although it wasn't particularly cold. "Will you leave her, then?" she said. Her gaze was out to sea.

"I've lasted this long."

"Becky might say the same."

"And she'd have a point."

"But something's changed, hasn't it? That's why you're here."

I made a face. "Perhaps something hasn't changed. Maybe that's the problem." Helen waited for me to go on. "I don't think I ever believed Becky was ill. Not really. I thought it was all her parents' fault. That she was a spoiled brat that just needed to grow up."

"And now?"

"I think I was right. Up to a point."

"But?"

I shrugged. "I suppose there's a bit more to it than that."

"It's taken you ten years to find that out?"

"The miscarriages didn't help."

"I don't suppose they would."

"They are still a smokescreen, though. Really."

"You have a way with words, John."

"I know how I sound sometimes."

"I'm not sure that you do." She sighed and let her shoulders relax. "But it's your choice, isn't it? If you leave or not."

"That would depend on how much of a bastard I am, wouldn't it?" She looked at me quizzically. "What sort of man leaves his wife because he realises that she's mentally ill?"

"For you, John, it shouldn't be a problem." If the smile was meant to soften her words it failed miserably.

She walked me to my car. Just as she was about to leave I said, "Oh, I almost forgot. I saved a man's life last night."

She tipped her head to one side. "That's such bullshit."

"Seriously."

I told her about the incident with Luke, leaving out any bits that made me sound bad. When I finished I looked into her face.

"You don't believe me."

She nodded slowly. "I don't think you've got the imagination to make it up."

I couldn't read her expression. "It's not as though I did much. I don't think he was going to jump anyway."

"You stopped, though. You could have walked on. Like Charlie, like the others. That means something."

"I suppose." I realised I was blushing. As I stared at the pavement Helen leaned forward and kissed my cheek.

"You did a good thing, John."

Then she left.

I drove back to Norwich and after lunch killed most of the afternoon in the Ladbrokes on Ber Street. I lost the best part of two hundred pounds backing favourites then won most of it back on a long shot in the last from Lingfield. It's always good to end on a winner. I finished the afternoon a few quid down but I felt as though I'd won.

I got home at the same time as I would if I'd been to work. Becky was on the sofa, drinking tea. Luke was sitting next to her.

When he saw me he jumped up and flung his arms open wide. "Here's the guy!"

Becky smiled at me. Her hair glistened as though freshly washed. "You should have told me, John."

I thought Luke was going to hug me but he settled for a handshake. "You're so modest," he gushed. "I've just been telling your lovely wife what a hero you are."

It was hard to believe it was the same man. He wore a mauve cord shirt that hung over the top of a pair of too-tight jeans. His features, so bland and immobile the previous night, were now absurdly animated. His voice was knowing and arch.

"What are you doing here?"

"Why, saying thank you, of course." His face was all innocent incredulity. But something else glimmered underneath. "I rushed off last night. It was thoughtless."

"How did you find me?"

"Don't be so rude, John." Becky was by my side. Her voice was soft, her eyes mild as she looked at me. She linked an arm through mine. She smelled faintly of peaches. "You did a wonderful thing. He just wants to thank you, that's all."

"It was nothing," I said.

Luke snorted, "Nothing. Right."

"He told me, John. You risked your life. Reached over the edge of the bridge and pulled him off."

"So to speak," Luke said. He shot an awful, hammy wink in Becky's direction. She giggled. I couldn't remember the last time I heard her giggle. I wanted to hit her.

I said, "That's not quite…"

"And he told me about Charlie."

"Not that I'm blaming him," Luke said. "In his place, I'd have done the same thing."

Becky tutted. "I doubt it, Luke," she said.

I looked at them both and wondered what planet they were on.

"Look, this is great and thanks for coming, but I'm hungry and…"

Luke held up a hand. "Of course. I'm sorry. It's just I'm going to tell the local paper about you. I wanted to make sure you don't mind."

"What?"

He gave a little smile. I didn't like it much. "The Evening News loves stuff…"

"No."

He looked hurt, or pretended to. "John," Becky said.

"I mean, you do whatever you need to do, but leave me out of it. I'm no hero."

"Your call," Luke said. "Shame, though."

We stood for a moment, the three of us. Becky looked crestfallen.

I said, "So what's your story, Luke?" He looked at me quizzically, didn't say anything. "Why were you there last night. What changed your mind, besides my heroics? I'm curious. I really am."

"I've intruded enough." The campness had gone from his voice.

"Dinner can wait. I'll make some more tea and you can tell us all about it."

"John," Becky said again, less indulgently this time.

Luke kissed Becky's hand. "I must go."

I followed him towards the hallway. Becky started after us but I raised a hand, stopping her. She went back into the living room and fussed with the furniture.

At the door Luke said, "How was the coast today? Did the fog clear?"

I was closing the door after him but now I hesitated.

"I just wondered," he said.

I felt Becky behind me. "Coast?" she said.

“I was at work,” I said.

I looked back at Luke and he was at the gate. He shot me a wink. “Be seeing you.”

I closed the door.

“I told you to wait in the living room.”

“I wanted to say goodbye to Luke.” Her eyes were trembling and wet at the edges.

In the kitchen I said, “You haven’t even started dinner.”

“I’ve had company. I’ve got to wash the tea things up. Put them away. You know that, John.” She was whining. She came up to me, pawed at my chest.

“How long was he here?”

“An hour or so. He phoned just after lunch and…”

“Phoned? How did he get our number?”

She locked her hands behind my neck and squirmed against me. “I don’t know. Does it matter?”

“And you let him in? He could have been anyone.”

“But he was lovely, John. And the things he said about you…”

I touched her blouse, her hair, her face. “You’re wearing make up. You’ve washed your hair. Is that for Luke’s benefit or for mine?”

She tried to hold me. “Yours, of course. I’m so proud of you.”

I pushed her away and searched the fridge and cupboards for food.

“I’ll fix us something,” Becky said.

“Forget it,” I grabbed a beer from the fridge, opened it and stomped into the living room.

Becky followed me. “Why are you so angry? You can’t be jealous. Luke’s gay. I thought even you might have noticed that.”

I turned on her. “And did the lovely Luke really strike you as a man on the brink of suicide?”

"He said that he's a manic depressive. I know about this stuff. The mood swings…"

"You know about what? You're not a manic depressive."

"No, but I've read…"

"You've read? Bloody wonderful." Her hand flew to her face and the first tears spilled onto her cheeks. "I wondered how long it would take."

She sat carefully on the edge of the sofa, leant forward with her knees together and composed herself. "I don't understand this, John. You did a wonderful thing. You saved a man's life. The thought of it made me feel…I don't know…warm, grateful. I couldn't wait for you to get home. To be honest, I didn't think you were capable of something like that."

She looked up at me and her eyes were dry again. I forced myself to breath evenly, made my voice gentler, normal. "I didn't save anybodies life, Becky. I stopped. I talked to him. But he never had any intention of jumping. I'm not a hero."

"He said you grabbed him."

"He's lying. I don't know why. Perhaps this is a game to him. I don't understand. I don't want to understand." She looked at me blankly. "The Luke you met today was nothing like the Luke on the bridge last night."

"What the hell are you talking about?"

"I know how it sounds…"

"I thought I was the loon."

I let out a long breath, ran a hand through my hair. "You're not to see him or talk to him again. Do you understand?"

She looked at me for a long time without speaking.

I woke in the middle of the night to find Becky straddling me. She was leant over me, a hand planted either side of my head. Strands of her hair brushed against my cheek.

I breathed slowly and looked up at her, waiting for my eyes to become used to the darkness. There was something feral in the way she was tensed over me and in her expression, as her features became clear, the curl of her lips exposing the tips of her incisors. Her eyes were hooded, mostly hidden by her hair.

Her breath was shocking. I thought of how clean she'd seemed the previous day, of the sweetness of her scent. It was as though she had decayed from the inside out in a matter of hours.

Eventually I said, "I'm a bit tired, love. And it's not even the first Saturday of the month."

She was wearing pyjamas, but even if she'd been naked the situation would have been less than erotic. We had made love in the position we were frozen in often enough in the past. It was one of my favourites. But that was then; a mythical, nebulous time. Possibly years ago. Or months. Or never.

"Would you have saved me, John?" Becky said. I turned my head to one side so that her breath slid past my cheek.

"What are you talking about?"

"Would you have stopped for me? Would you have pulled me away from the edge?"

"I didn't pull…"

"You showed more compassion towards a man you'd never met before than you have ever shown to me."

Her voice was flat and calm and matter of fact. What she said was wrong on several levels. She also had a point.

I put my hand on the back of her head and pulled her face towards me. Her lips parted and I slid my tongue into her mouth. The taste was indescribably bad. But I didn't stop kissing her.

It the morning I assumed that it was a dream. Becky got up at the same time as I did and pottered around in the kitchen. She smelled fine and her breath was normal. I ate my breakfast, drank some coffee then stood under a hot shower for half an hour and tried to wash all thoughts of the previous night away.

As I was about to leave for work Becky kissed my cheek and said, "You know we didn't use any protection last night, don't you? And it's my fertile time."

I looked into her face but her expression was impossible to read.

That night I went to bed late, Becky was waiting for me with the bedside lamp on, reading. When I got into bed she curled against me. She was naked and her small breasts squeezed against my chest. She smelled of apples. When I kissed her I tasted Aquafresh and nothing else.

On Saturday evening I met Charlie at the Playhouse Bar. Neither of us mentioned the previous Sunday. Charlie's band had played a gig on Friday night and we chatted about that. After a while Charlie said, "What's up with you?"

"What?"

"We've been talking about the band for ten minutes and you haven't taken the piss."

I tried to shrug, but it was difficult in the crowded bar. "I would have got around to it."

"Really?" He squinted through the smoke. "I'm not so sure. You seem distinctly mellow. You're either stoned or you've been getting your end away for a change."

"You have such an elegant way with words."

"And you're not stoned, are you?" I shook my head. "So who's the lucky lady?"

"What the hell is that supposed to mean?"

"Easy," Charlie said. "I thought with your trip to the coast on Monday…"

I realised I'd pretty much forgotten about Helen. "That didn't quite work out."

"So we're talking about Becky?"

"*You* are talking about Becky. I'm not sure this any of your business."

"What the fuck has that got to do with anything?" He looked so indignant I almost smiled.

"Things are different. Better."

"What, in less than a week?" I could understand his incredulity. I had only ever moaned about my marriage in all the years I'd known him.

The music and the level of conversation were so loud we had to shout to make ourselves heard. I pointed in the vague direction of the door. "Shall we move on?"

Charlie nodded and we squeezed our way to the exit.

The Playhouse is set on the bank of the Wensum and we stood on the small bridge that crosses the river and looked out at the water. It was perfectly still and as dark as ink. The night was unseasonably warm. The air was heavy with a scent I couldn't quite place.

"So what happened?" Charlie said. "Have you found God? Has Becky found God?"

"Now who's taking the piss?"

"I'm sorry. It's just…"

"I know." I considered mentioning Luke then, but decided not to. I wasn't sure if he had anything to do with the change in Becky, in me, with the improvement in our relationship. But I didn't want to admit the possibility. Not to Charlie. Not to myself. "She's a bit better, that's all. She's off the medication. And she's looking after herself. You know, eating properly, washing, stuff like that."

"And you?"

"Dunno. I'm a bit more patient, I suppose. I try to listen to her, not just dismiss what she says out of hand."

"Big of you." His voice flattened and I remembered how he felt about Becky. I looked at him but he kept his eyes fixed on the river.

"I know it doesn't sound much…"

"Actually, it does." He gave a tight smile. "Good for you." I think he meant it.

"As you say, it's less than a week."

"But it's a start."

"It's a start," I agreed.

We walked past the Art College, some flats, a deli.

"What changed?" he said, as we turned right at a pub called Armstrong's, skirting a pair of bouncers in the process. The state of Armstrong's I thought they probably needed them to keep people in. "Why now?"

"Shall we go to the Ten Bell's?"

"Anything to do with that dude on the bridge?"

I stopped. "Why should it be?"

"I just wondered…"

"Don't."

He hesitated then said, "Did he jump? I didn't see anything in the papers, but…"

"No," I said. "He didn't jump."

Charlie nodded. We stood for a moment. Then he said, "Hey, you should have seen this chick last night. She so wanted me, man…"

We walked to the pub.

We found a corner table in the Ten Bells. I told Charlie about Helen and he shrugged and said he thought it was for the best. He was lying, of course. I think part of him always imagined Helen and I getting together, leaving him to save Becky. I'd probably had similar thoughts myself. Neither of us bothered to find out what Becky thought.

We spent half an hour discussing Charlie's love life. It was as complex and sordid as usual. Entertaining, though. Then we ticked the usual boxes; football, music, films. This led, as it always did, to Uma Thurman, who Charlie, inexplicably in my opinion, found irresistible.

By ten, though, I was getting restless. I realised I wanted to get home to Becky. Which was something of a first.

"You're turning into a lightweight," Charlie said. We stood on the pavement outside the Ten Bells.

I started to button my coat, decided against it. The night was milder still, far too warm for January.

"Could be," I said. I was pleasantly sober. Charlie had drunk considerably more than me and seemed vague and unfocused. I felt bad for him suddenly. "I'm sorry. I've buggered up your evening."

"Hey, the night's young," he said.

"That's right. Maybe you can scare up one of those women of yours. The list is long enough, after all."

"Always an option," he said. But his heart didn't appear to be in it. For a moment he looked lost, alone.

Then someone tapped me on the shoulder. I caught a whiff of sandalwood as I turned. Luke said, "Hi guys."

Charlie squinted at him. Then he pointed and started to say something, but instead Luke said to him, "Hey, no hard feelings. In your place I'd have done the same thing. We can't all be hero's like John here."

He was different again. All trace of campness had gone. His voice was loud and coarse. On the surface he appeared drunk, but I doubted that he was.

"We're just off," I said.

Luke clapped me on the shoulder and took a deep breath. "Odd weather, isn't it? And that smell. A bit like spunk. Like maybe God just had a wank."

A couple across the street turned to look and a big, bearded guy slowed as he passed and sneered into Luke's face.

"What is wrong with you?" I said.

"What?" Luke's eyes were wide open. "Don't act all offended, John. It's not as though you even believe in God."

"How the…"

"Don't bother denying it. How about you, Charlie? Do you believe in the Big Guy?"

"I believe you're a nut," Charlie said.

"But not a hypocrite, right? Not like you two." He was smiling. His voice was loud, but playful. "Lighten up. It's no big deal."

"What the fuck are you doing here?" I said.

"You're a hard man to find, John."

"Why are you…"

"I mean, Becky's a sweetheart, but…"

Before I could speak Charlie stepped past me and planted a hand on Luke's chest. "What about Becky?"

"Whoa," Luke said. He took a step back, his arms held wide. Everything about him seemed exaggerated, cartoon-like. Except the small, hard thing that glittered behind his eyes. "Easy, tiger. Becky's *his* wife. Am I right?"

Charlie drew back.

"What about Becky?" I said.

"We've had a couple of chats, that's all. Like I say; a sweetheart. By the look on your face you didn't get my messages?"

"Just say what you've got to say and fuck off."

He was close to me. He leant forward quickly and kissed me softly on the mouth. I was appalled but I didn't move. For a moment I thought I tasted something dark and foul. That may have been my imagination. Luke took a couple of steps backwards. His eyes shone with a lunatic light. He grinned enormously, as though he'd told a fantastic joke and I was the punch line.

Charlie tried to go for him but I held him back. Luke laughed once then turned and ran.

I wiped my mouth again and again.

Charlie said, "Jesus Christ."

I said nothing.

Charlie said, "Is he fucking around with Becky?"

"I don't know. I'll find out. I'll sort it."

Before he left me Charlie said, "Last Sunday? Still glad you stopped?"

"Sure," I said. "I'm glad I stopped. It's not giving the fucker a push that I regret."

I found Becky in the living room. She stood by an armchair, manoeuvring it a millimetre at a time.

"It's fine," I said.

"It isn't," she said. Her voice was small and intense. Her eyes were fixed on the chair as she tried to get it into exactly the right position.

"Sit down," I said.

"Not yet." She wore her black silk kimono and her hair was wet. Her face was rapt with concentration. She hadn't looked at me since I'd walked through the door.

"I know he called." I tried to keep my voice light, conversational. My mouth burned where Luke kissed me.

It was as though she hadn't heard me. She stood upright, backed away from the chair, squinting at it through her hands, like an artist getting a scene into perspective. "That's better."

"Becky," I said.

Her eyes flicked around the room, seeking out other inconsistencies. "I didn't speak to him. I just put the phone down."

"Why didn't you tell me?"

"I thought you'd be angry. You said I mustn't talk to him. But I didn't talk to him. I put the phone down." Her voice was flatter than the Fens. The words chopped up, laid out in a line.

"He said something about a message."

Her eyes were as large as a child's as they found mine. "No."

"You mean…"

"He didn't leave a message."

"Ok."

"You believe me, don't you?"

"Of course."

"Don't you?" Again, as though I hadn't spoken. She stood with her hands clenched together in front of her. Her whole body quivered.

I wondered where the real Becky had gone; the Becky I'd held the night before and who'd held me back. The one I'd looked forward to coming home to. Perhaps this was the real Becky. It's not as though I've ever really known.

I stepped forward, held her shoulders gently. "Of course I believe you, Becky."

She started crying.

I held her for as long as she'd let me, which wasn't long, and then we sat at opposite ends of the sofa.

"You should go to bed," I said. "You look exhausted."

"Can't. My hair's still wet." She ran a hand through it absently.

"Why did you wash it so late?"

"You like it clean, you said. When it smells nice. I washed it five times today, just to be sure."

I stood. "I'll get us some hot chocolate, then. While we wait for it to dry."

I must have moved the sofa slightly because when I brought our drinks into the living room she was still trying to get it back into position.

I woke late. My head felt thick and woolly, as though I'd drunk heavily or been drugged. Becky sat on the edge of the bed, watching me. She was dressed. There was something in the calculated emptiness of her expression that frightened me a little.

"What time is it?" I said.

"Just after ten."

After a moment I said, "What is it?"

"Luke was here."

I sat up. "When?"

"A little while ago."

I slid out of bed and started to dress. Becky's gaze remained on my pillow, as though I hadn't moved at all. "Why didn't you wake me?"

"He told me not to." Her voice was matter of fact. I felt old and slow and stupid. I tried to think but found that it hurt so I stopped. Easier to accept that nothing made sense anymore. I started to look for a clean shirt, then realised I didn't give a shit so I slipped on the one I'd worn the day before.

"He kissed me," Becky said.

"What?" I stopped buttoning my shirt. I put my hand on her chin and tilted her head until she faced me.

Her eyes widened as she saw the expression on my face. "I couldn't stop him. It was just a peck. That's all." She wrinkled her nose. "It tasted…bad."

I thought of how quick he'd been the previous night. I let my hand drop from her face. "What else did he do?"

"Nothing. Honestly. I thought he was going to, for a moment, at least. I suppose he could have done. He had me backed against the wall in the hallway."

"Why didn't you shout?"

"He told me not to. I was scared, John."

The spaced-out vagueness that had enveloped her the night before seemed to have gone. I supposed that was a good thing. I was no longer sure.

"I've been sat on the bed for the last hour, waiting for you to wake up."

"Why did you wait, Becky?"

Her head dipped and I stroked her hair. "I'm scared of you too, John."

I sat on the bed and held her.

We went downstairs. I put my coat on.

"Where are you going?" Becky said.

"I'd better try and find him. Or go to the police. I can't just leave…"

She grabbed my sleeve. "It's ok. I think we've seen the last of him."

"Why?"

"After…after he kissed me he said that he was sorry. That was why he came round. To apologise. To both of us."

"Right. So why didn't he let you wake me?"

"He couldn't face you, he said."

I grunted.

"I believe him, John. Really. He said that someone he loved had died suddenly, violently. He couldn't get over it. He wasn't himself, he said. He thought we'd both like the real Luke."

"I somehow doubt it. Was that it?"

She shrugged and smiled. "Pretty much. He ran on a bit about this girl, about how they used to go for walks along Cromer beach, drink coffee on the front. I mean, winter beaches, how original. I don't know…"

Her smile froze when she saw my face. "This girl. Did he mention a name?"

"Yeah. She was called Helen. Why?"

It was raining hard when I parked on a double yellow line a few doors down from Helen's house. I'd tried her mobile every five minutes during the drive to Cromer but could only reach her voicemail. Becky had let me go without a word. I kissed her cold cheek and said I'd explain when I got home. She didn't look as though she believed me. I didn't blame her.

I was half-soaked by the time I got to Helen's door. I knocked hard ten or twelve times but got no reply. I stood on the step and stared at the bright red door as if it might give me some sort of clue what to do next.

Something caught my peripheral vision and I turned my head to the right to see two figures, blurred by the rain, approaching hesitantly. They stopped as they reached the gate and I turned to face them.

"John?" Helen said as she pulled the hood of her anorak down. Her blond hair was immediately drenched and flattened against her scalp.

It was an immense relief to see her. I also felt utterly, exquisitely stupid.

It was Dominic she was with, obviously. I didn't hang around long enough to even get a look at him. I just mumbled an apology, ignored the look of concerned bemusement on Helen's face and got the fuck out of there.

It was uncomfortable driving home. My clothes were soaked and, consequently, so was the driver's seat. The inside of the windscreen kept fogging up. All I could seem to find on the radio was a political debate or something about gardening or music by some bloody boy band or other.

When my mobile rang I thought it would be a welcome distraction. I was wrong.

"Did you really think I'd hurt her?" Luke said.

After a moment I said, "What am I supposed to think?"

"That's cold, John."

"Can we stop this now? You told Becky it was over..."

"Sweet Becky. She'll believe anything, won't she? Quite endearing, really. There's a bit of chemistry there, believe me. Between Becky and I. No offence, of course."

"There's something missing, isn't there, Luke? Maybe you were dropped on the head as a baby, maybe...well, whatever. We'll just agree you need help. But that's not my problem. But I promise you, bother us again and I'll find you and I'll shove your head so far up your fucking arse..."

"I'm trembling, John. I'm all a quiver." His voice dropped to a whisper. "She doesn't know about Helen, does she?"

I said nothing. I wanted to ask if he'd told her. I wanted to beg him not to. I did neither. The rain was so hard now I could hardly see where I was going. I pulled over to the side of the road and turned the engine off.

"That's pretty poor, John. What's a relationship without trust, without honestly?"

"Why are you doing this? I…saved your life. I stopped, at least." I heard my own voice, judged how pathetic it sounded and mentally shot myself in the head.

"I know." He sounded different again. I thought I heard something in the background. "It's nearly over." His voice flat-lined and I felt the hairs on my neck stiffen. "We're getting to the vinegar strokes now, John."

Again I thought I heard something. A voice maybe, muffled.

"Where are you?" I said.

The line hissed for a moment then he broke the connection.

I started the car again and pulled onto the road without checking for oncoming traffic.

When I got home Becky had gone. I flailed around the empty house looking for her. As though she might be hiding in a cupboard. Upstairs I found that most of her clothes were missing along with all of her underwear. But her medication was still in the bathroom cabinet and, in the tumbler on the hand basin, her pink toothbrush leant against mine.

There was a note on the coffee table on the living room. It said simply, "I know". Becky had signed her name with an 'i'.

The room smelled faintly of sandalwood. The sofa and one of the armchairs were at least six inches out of position.

My adult mind spoke to me in a quiet, sane voice. It told me that everything could be easily explained. It reminded me gently of the things I had to do. Practical things; like calling the police and speaking to Becky's parents. That was where she'd be, the voice told me. Almost certainly.

As these thoughts continued, mannered and reasonable, I ran out of the front door into the indifferent rain. I stopped at the gate. I grabbed hold of the cold metal and called her name again and again.

Certain Faces

Stephen Volk

In memory of Melanie Hall

One

I wake feeling lost and scared, not scissoring upright like in a cheap horror film, but filled with the dull, heavy dread that another day has begun, a day no different and no easier than the one that went before. I wake more tired than when my head hit the pillow. I feel like a lump of lead and someone will drop me in a pool of water, and that's the day, and that's me going through the day, till I hit the bottom. Then it all happens over again. I twist to see the clock radio on the floor which reads a red 6.30 and I pick up my Annie Proulx and start to read. Except I don't read, I go over the same page three, four times without taking it in. I'm not awake and I'm not asleep. I'm buzzing. My husband opens an eye, the other sunk deep in the pillow. His grunt is warm, groggy, inquisitorial. Eventually I drop the book beside the bed and turn onto my side and try to sleep again. I'm staring at his back and waiting for the alarm while a figure of eight of predictable thoughts knot my stomach like food poisoning. I wish that's what it was. And this part lasts forever, the thinking, tell him, tell him, tell him. The thinking, which is worse? Not telling my husband, or not telling the police?

As per usual, I'm just falling deep asleep when the alarm drills into me. It makes me ratty. Gavin wakes now, well-slept and fresh and I'm angry at him, envious. He knows I've been awake, I always have. I can't help it. It's my body clock. I can take a nap in the afternoon, no problem. He never can. He says there are too many things to worry about in the daytime.

We're all legs and arms on the sofa bed in the main room, like unwanted stopovers in our own home. He's been decorating the bedroom, orange, scarlet, navy blue, my idea, and the closed door doesn't keep out the smell of turps. He sits at the end of the bed with his long curved white back and grabs the remote control and an ashtray and switches on breakfast TV. I find my nose with my specs and see one of those big-mouthed presenters with microscopic tits and a tight lime green shirt.

"I hate that bloody woman," he says, the cigarette waggling between his lips.

I say, "What's she done to you?"

The lighter clicks. He puffs. "Nothing. Look at the state of her. Jesus."

I say, "Eamonn Holmes is no oil painting."

"Those lips," he says. "They're abnormal."

"Switch it fucking off then," I say.

I don't expect him to, but he does, his back still to me. It's like someone pulls the plug on the room.

I say, "Joking."

In the silence, he acts like he hasn't heard me.

His weight lifts from the bed and he heads for the bathroom and I cross the bed on all fours and pick up the remote control and turn it back on.

"Gavin. Don't be an idiot. Christ."

I hear him close the bathroom door. "I'm having a shit. Is that all right?"

I turn up the volume. The girl on TV is wearing more lipstick than I put on in a week. I pull the sheets up over my knees. If my Gran in Aberdeen didn't like someone on TV, she wouldn't switch off, she'd talk to them. She'd tell them to bugger off, silly sods. Or she'd cover her head with a tea cloth so she wouldn't have to see them. When I got my A-level results and got into Art College, she ran down the hall to hug me, waddling like an oversized hair-netted baby.

As I open my knicker drawer, I wonder if Vicki Hartwell had a Gran who hugged her when she got into college, who had tears running down her cheeks over her A-levels, as if that was the last thing she had to worry about in the world, her granddaughter's life would be fine.

I sometimes wonder how it happened between Gavin and me. How does it happen between anyone, I suppose? All I remember is needing a fireplace taking out because I was desperate to flog it for the money, and someone recommended this guy who was a builder who'd been to Art College, like me. We got on, but we didn't say that much. He was what my Mum called quiet spoken. There wasn't any roughness about him. One night we shared a bottle of wine and I got weepy. It was a hard time in my life. We went to bed and before I knew it he was spending two, three nights a week with me. It was just natural. He didn't seem bothered I had a grown-up daughter. Then when I said I wanted to move away from Edinburgh he said, "Aye, why not?" and before I knew it, we were buying a flat together down south. After a bit he said he wanted to get married, which was nice to hear. I laughed, but it was really nice. Maybe he felt it was time to eradicate my past, give it a new coat of paint. I don't know.

I'm always first up, first dressed and watered, first to rummage in the bread bin. The toaster's chirruping like a time bomb and Gavin hasn't emerged from the bathroom. When he does, I slam the cutlery drawer and say, "I'm sick of making the *fucking* breakfast every morning. Why is it me that has to do everything around here?" Now he sulks, like a little boy who's had his legs slapped. He thinks things like this bother me, but they don't, not really.

I want him to answer back, but he doesn't. I want him to yell at me, but he doesn't. He comes up behind me and rubs my arms and plants a kiss on my neck. I don't move. I empty a carton of three day-old milk down the sink.

I realise I have my hand over my stomach. I don't know why. It's like someone else put it there.

Gavin dresses, in the tartan lumberjack shirt I bought him for his birthday but is now only worth working in. Says he'll be in The Fox at seven. That's a novelty.

I say, "Let's not make it The Fox."

He says, "Where do you want to make it?"

"Anywhere. Nowhere. I don't care."

"OK. Forget it."

He knows I want a slanging match. I want him to suffer today. I want him to suffer instead of me.

But he doesn't play the game. He doesn't even slam the door. His Silk Cut lies recumbent in the ashtray on the corner of the bath and I prod it till the smoke stops rising. There's an anorexic girl from Marie Claire on the floor, advertising shoes. I sit on the broken loo seat, forearms strapping my ribs, feeling them ache and heave and the desert-dry saltiness spreads out from my sinuses, and I'm crying, and it doesn't surprise me any more.

Vicki Hartwell was completely forgettable. I would have forgotten her in five minutes I think, if things had been different. She wouldn't have stuck in my mind, visually, or any other way, really.

She was one of these people who's never had a problem, probably, getting a boyfriend, because she has a pretty face. But she's never stood out either, because there's nothing unusual about her face either. She was completely conventional and completely boring.

Having said that, she was very confident with the way she looked. She knew she looked all right, and maybe that's what put me off her. I wish I had her confidence. I actually like people who are slightly nervy, insecure, I don't know why. It might be because I want to feel in a stronger position because I'm the one that's having to paint them, and I don't want to feel like the shy one. So it could be to do with that, but it's more than that. I think I like people with flaws, it reassures me. People who don't show flaws, who are all front, I find that frightening, people with no self doubt. I don't think anybody's really without doubts and fears. Some people cover it up, that's all. Cover it up well, that's the thing. I can't relate to someone who's really confident, 100% confident, 100% of the time.

What attracts me? Usually, it's an interestingly shaped head. Usually that's the connection with the short hair. Also, I do like men who have a sensitive, feminine look about them. It can be very well hidden, but it is there. And I like women again who have a boyish masculine side to them as well. I like people to have a bit of both. I think that's probably why I didn't like Vicki Hartwell, because she was too "girly." It was too one-dimensional. There was no more to find out. There was too much oestrogen there, just like with some guys there's too much testosterone flying around.

I suppose what I'm looking for is a nice combination. That's why you'll find pictures all over my studio of Michael Clark, DV8, k.d. lang. Because I think we all have both, and if you can get both, it's probably one of the strongest requirements.

At the beginning I was naive. I used to ask people to come round and I'd struggle to paint them, and it wasn't right, and I'd have to pay them, which was mad. So I got in the habit of meeting them first in some neutral zone, and I always said beforehand, "Please don't be offended if I can't use you, because it's nothing to do with prettiness or attractiveness, it's just that I personally can't use you." And, apart from what happened with Vicki, that usually works out fine.

Two

The one who phoned me was this guy Emyr Winter. I

remember because he had to spell it because I thought he said Emma, a girl's name. I said "Sorry." I was still flustered from rushing to catch the answerphone from cutting in. I said, "Yes, this is the real me. This is not a machine."

There was pub noise in the background. The sound of the smell of sticky floors. Then this kangarooing Welsh accent, quite high, quite nervous. "I'm – er, ringing about the card you put in the Metro Cafe? Sitter stroke model required by professional female artist?"

"That's right. That's me."

"We were – my friend and me, were wondering like, what's *involved* exactly?"

He made *involved* sound like some long drawn-out gynaecological word. I wondered if he was going to be one of those ones who thought the word model was some euphemism for blow job, but then I thought, you can't go by a voice, he might have a brilliant head, and that's what I'm after, so I leaned against the wall, looking back at Gavin slumped in front of *Parkinson* with a San Miguel balanced on one knee, and said what I usually say: "Well, you sit, in a chair, clothed, by the way, and I paint you. Heads. Heads and shoulders, that's all I'm interested in. Don't worry. I'm not after your body." That was my usual line, to put people at ease.

The penny dropped, literally. Two gobbits of change gulped up by the payphone, and the pub ambience cut back in, laughter, but not from him. Had he heard what I'd said? "That sounds all right, then. Nothing too drastic."

"Nothing drastic at all."

A voice muttered impatiently in the background amongst the chinked glasses.

He asked about the pay.

"Well, it isn't a fortune. Four pounds an hour. You'd get more babysitting." I heard him cover the mouthpiece and relay it. I imagined facial expressions.

"That's orright. There are three of us interested,

actually..."

"Great. Well, I'll have to have a look at you."

He said his flatmate's name was Paul Rolt who had a girlfriend called Vicki. He said they were all students at the University up on Coombe Down. At that point I took it all three of them shared. It was only afterwards, from the Chronicle, I found out that Vicki lived with her parents in Colerne. But that was the impression I got, that they were students and they all lived together in Bath.

"I'll have to have a look at you. You might not all be – you know, suitable..."

"Suitable?"

"Well, you know. I have certain requirements, certain types I'm looking for. They're not strictly portraits, they're more imaginative. They represent me, what's going on in my head, as much as anything." I realised I was sounding pretentious, so I shut up.

"Oh, yes. Well you're the artist, you know what you're doing," he said. "So when would you want us to come round and pose, exactly?" I remember he used the word *pose*, which I hate, but I suppose it's a word normal people use.

"Well," I said. "What if we meet up first?"

"Only, like I say, we're all at the University. Would it be in the evenings? Only, the day might be awkward like."

"Let's talk about that when we meet up, shall we?"

"Oh, oh. OK. Right. Fine."

I suggested the Metro Cafe, since they knew it, at 11.30 the following morning, a Sunday. I said they did a good all-day breakfast, and he said they'd have to give that a test-drive, he looked forward to that.

The last thing he said was, "You'll know us because we'll all be sitting together, there'll be three of us. And Paul and I have got short hair."

So I thought, that means nothing. I said, "You'll know me because I'll be covered in paint."

This bloke Emyr laughed, like it was a joke.

Three

When I walked into the Metro Cafe on the Sunday morning I walked right past them. I didn't even notice them, they were that interesting.

I don't know what I was expecting. I used to live in a gay area of Edinburgh and I had terrific models from a semi-gay cafe called Fat Tuesday: three, four different models a week. The Metro, with its Parisian *Eurotrash* cum bombed-out barbershop look, maroon woodwork and fake marble effect walls, freaky found objects, and Gwen Stefani blaring out of the speakers, or Kaiser Chiefs, or Moby, had the same mix of clientele; young, gay, poseurs. Even the layabouts looked like Rufus Wainwright. It attracted the type I liked. Shaven heads, nose rings, tattoos, a certain beatnik, punkish, retro, androgynous, that Blade Runner, Bjork, Michael Stipes, Calvin Klein junkie-chic. It was perfect. The perfect trawling ground, the perfect wateringhole. So when they said students, I expected the same, only more so: hip, wacky, slight off-beat, slightly sexy in whatever way, I don't care.

One of them must have seen I was wearing this baggy shirt splattered in paint, because a man's voice behind me sing-songed, "Be-hind yoo!" And I turned and thought – as soon as I set eyes on them – shit, you're not right, no, none of you are right at all. They were dead boring looking.

"Oh hi there," I heard myself saying. "Nice to meet you." I couldn't believe there was this great big grin on my face as I shook hands with the three of them and pulled a chair under me as I was introduced to them. Hi, hi, hi. At that stage I was thinking, I just want to get out of here, I just want to terminate it here and now and go. I wanted to say look, thank you, sorry, but goodbye.

They were all smoking, especially this Vicki girl, who was

I suppose pretty in a very conventional, conservative, *Bride & Home* kind of way. I could see her walking down the aisle, that's what she was made for, I thought, that's all she wants in life. I'm not saying you couldn't tick all the boxes, sure. Round face, pointed chin, a child-like smile which seemed to nudge her cheek bones higher, waves of Barbie-doll ginger hair which you could see were her crowning glory, shampooed twice a day and dried for three hours, groomed to oblivion. Even the occasional shy, girlie, toss of the head. But there was nothing natural there. It was all received wisdom, *Baywatch*, Fergie, Tatler sort of beauty, a copycat creation, something manufactured for men, an advertisement, not a person with anything underneath, and ultimately banal, like someone who works in a building society and everyone tells her she should be a model, and she believes them.

She took off her dark glasses and said, "Sorry we're a bit..." and poked out her tongue and rolled her dull eyes. "There was this party over in Larkhall and they got into the tequilas. I have got *such* a hangover you wouldn't believe it. I don't even remember walking home. I remember this water pistol fight, but that's about all. We're all a weeny bit..." She gritted her teeth sheepishly in place of a word and fluttered her eyelids. I don't know if I was supposed to be impressed or something. I thought she sounded like an idiot.

"Delicate," said the Welsh one. "Green around the gills."

"How Green Were My Gills," said the other guy, her boyfriend, Paul, standing up, taking off his own shades. "Have you ordered anything?" I said yes, a cappuccino, and he did some semaphore to the waiter pointing down at my head giving the thumbs up. He had a South African accent and tree trunk legs in shorts, like an overgrown little boy, with a greasy Beatle cut like you get on Lego people.

I just felt instantly this was a waste of time. Two of them weren't physically right, and the third one, this Emyr, who might have been physically a possibility, wasn't right personality wise. He was like Tintin. He had fifteen layers of clothes on, all too big for him. The shirt label on the back of his neck stuck up like a flag. I could have painted him, but he kept staring at his shoes, he just seemed incredibly bashful. I don't actually think he could have managed a sitting. I think he would have had a panic attack.

Vicki sat with her back to the brightly sunlit street. They had a Sunday Times pulled limb from limb all over the table top, and their ashtray was already a grey, spilling crematorium. She said, "I suppose one day we'll be able to say to our grandkids, there we were in that café chatting to that famous artist. And see that picture on the wall? That's your Gran, that is."

The others chuckled.

"In the National Gallery, aye," I said. "I don't think so."

"You don't think you'll be famous?"

I shrugged. "I don't think this is exactly the Deux Magots, is it?"

Emyr looked up from his trainers. "What's that when it's at home?"

"It's a skin disease," said Paul. "Like dermatitis."

"It's that cafe in Paris where Picasso hung out," I said. "And Albert Camus. And Sartre, I think. You know. That existentialist lot."

"No," said Emyr with an uninflected honesty. "Not really," and looked back at his shoes.

"Emyr's studying Oceanography," said Paul. "Floating little boat shaped things in tanks of water and looking at screens going blip, blip, blip."

"And what are you studying?" I asked Vicki.

"Beauty technology," she said without any visible irony, leaning forward to allow some ash to be rolled off her cigarette tip. "Part time."

"Political science," said Paul.

"You come from the right country for it," I said.

"I do," he said. "Where did you study? You did study, I presume."

"Aberdeen."

He raised both eyebrows.

"And the Royal College."

He blew smoke.

"Of Art."

He nodded and brushed non-existent ash from his knee. My cappuccino came, with a Virgin Mary for Vicki. She blinked a lot I noticed, like the cigarette fug she chimneyed irritated her own eyes, or she needed glasses and was too vain to wear them. She never seemed to completely focus. It may have been that she was suffering from some allergenic pollution due to the mascara she wore. All three were equal possibilities.

"It must be really really difficult, and that." *And that.* She had a Wiltshire accent, but probably thought she sounded like a newsreader. "I mean finding the motivation. You must be incredibly self-disciplined. I mean, without a boss, without clocking on, without a wage packet, getting up and getting down to painting away every day."

"Not really. I have to earn a living. I've got a mortgage to pay like everybody else. It's not a hobby, it's not for fun – it's a job."

"But you must love what you do, though."

I made a face. "Sometimes. Not all the time. Not when it's not going well. When it's going like shit, it can be hell. I hate it."

I could see she didn't understand that at all. "But at least you're expressing yourself. You're lucky. Most people don't get a chance to do that."

"Everyone can make marks on paper, to a certain extent, if they want to enough. Everyone can draw. I don't believe in this bollocks that you're born with it, like some gift. You don't talk about a plumber having a gift, or a doctor. You work at it. I work at it bloody hard. Through the night, sometimes, seven days a week. It makes me laugh. It doesn't flow effortlessly from your fingertips and there's a masterpiece, like people seem to think."

"That's not what I meant."

"No, sorry, I'm just saying that's what a lot of people think."

"Well, most people are ignorant, aren't they?"

I was waiting for it, and true enough, she said she'd always been artistic. Her Dad said she was drawing all the time, as a kid.

"Oh," I said. "You weren't tempted to take it further?"

She curled up her nose, tilted her head. I thought, *you really are a very thick person.*

Paul said, "At least you don't work for anybody, you don't have anybody breathing down your neck."

I laughed. "Tell my gallery that."

"So do you rate Picasso then?" said Vicki. "I mean, what they say, do you think he's a proper painter? I mean, to some people, he just splashes it all over, all this abstract what-not."

"Well, it's an acquired taste, I suppose. I'm not sure I got into it before Art College. If you start to work with problems on canvas you start to see what it's all about, but you shouldn't feel inadequate if you don't appreciate it."

"I don't feel inadequate," Vicki said. "I just think it's taking the piss. It's as simple as that. You know, squiggling something and selling it for ten thousand quid, it's ridiculous that is. You can buy a car for that."

"You're probably right," I said. Thinking, hey, I didn't do five years of Art School to go fifteen rounds on Picasso's blue period with a beauty therapist.

"What about opera?" said Paul. "What do you think of that?" Like they were all in the same airy-fairy bag.

I didn't know what to say. "I don't know much about opera, to be honest."

"You can still give an opinion," he said. "Can't you?" He was looking at me. Not staring, but looking.

"I don't know, to be honest." I tried to say something funny. "Load of fattish women singing about dying of consumption most of the time."

He didn't laugh. "She doesn't know," he said slowly, still looking at me, his eyes not moving from me.

Then Vicki Hartwell said, "How much money do you make? Not being rude or anything. Just curious."

I thought, put it like this, I'm not jetting off to the south of France. I'm not jetting off anywhere unless I get another exhibition or Gavin builds an extension pretty sharpish. I figetted and licked the froth off of the back of my spoon and said, "It varies."

"Enough to make a living though?" said Emyr. "Occasionally." I laughed again.

I don't know why.

Vicki said "Look, I expect you'll want to see these. I brought them along anyway." She lifted up these hefty WH Smith albums with tissue paper out of a Threshers carrier bag, and stacked them on the table. "They'll give you some ideas. Won't they Paul?"

I leafed through the photograph albums, delicately, as if they were aged Bibles that might crumble to the touch. "That's from a holiday me and Paul went on to the Seychelles. Have you been to the Seychelles?" I shook my head like a dunce. "Love-ly," she said dreamily. "*Love*-ly..."

My eyes flickered back down to bikini shots with a thong tight up the crack of her behind. Topless ones showing off the off-white breasts against a gravy-coloured tan. Back-lit shots, with her legs apart in the waves. The tossed hair of a Page Three Girl.

She arched back her head and blew smoke.

"She's not shocked," Vicki nudged Emyr's arm. "She's seen a lot more than that in Art College. A *heck* of a lot more.

"I bet," said Emyr, his head level with his chest.

I leafed through the rest, robotic now, playing the game but not really looking. There was something dirty about them, vaguely sleazy and intrusive. Private. A bathroom shot, after the suntan oil. The white rim above boxer shorts lowered an inch. Naked in the pool, floating strawberries of nipples under the scummy aquamarine. I could see she thought that was somehow artistic and that I would understand, that there was common ground. Legs apart, bent over. 18-30 meets Readers' Wives. I could see the pale, soft line of her bikini wax. I couldn't wait to hand them back.

"Good photographs."

What else could I say?

She looked at me and gave a little shrug, like she knew that already. "My boyfriend's a good photographer. He's got talent. He did my friend Stacy's wedding, everybody said his pictures were better than the professional's." She leaned across and kissed Paul on the cheek, and ran her hand down his thigh. He grinned like a petted Labrador.

"There you go," I said.

"David Bailey," said her boyfriend, miming a camera and clicking the shutter.

"There was this little bar run by English people, they were ever so nice. They said it was a change not to talk about the Royal Family or British beef. They opened this big bottle of Calvados. We got *such* a hangover that night, it's not true. I felt like somebody hit me over the head. I couldn't lift my head out of the pillow for two days."

I was thinking to myself, she's very proud of her breasts. She is very proud of the fact that men like her breasts.

Then Vicki Hartwell asked me, "What kind of painting do you do?"

I never know how to answer that, so I mumbled about the BP Award and they nodded as if they'd heard of it, which they obviously hadn't. If I said I'm influenced by Egon Shiele or

John Kirby or Ken Currie they'd be thinking I'm this bighead artist showing off, so I said "Figures and heads," embarrassed-sounding and annoyed at myself for being like that. (Then I thought, who are these people, anyway? Why should I worry what they think? I just want to get out of here. I just want to see the bottom of this cappuccino cup.)

I put another spoonful of sugar in, and I could tell Vicki was thinking, Oh yeah, she could afford to shed a couple of pounds around the hips, in those leggings.

"The card is one of mine," I said, and went and fetched the old Private View invite still blue-tacked to the imitation Louis Whatever mirror with my number written on it. I passed it round. They obviously hadn't looked at it that closely.

Vicki said, "Is it a good likeness?"

"Not really."

Emyr said, "Has he really got a neck that long?"

"Artistic license isn't it?" said the smug boyfriend. "Does he really have a dappled, blotchy face with red and green bits all over it?"

I said, "Not really."

"Do you know what it looks like?" he said, holding it. "A penis. The long neck, look. The head at the top with the red cheeks and the shiny head like a glans. It's like an *engorged* penis. Is that intentional?" He had a little cut under one eye, as if someone had bashed him. He had whiskers breaking through an erupting splatter of pimples. "Or is that my dirty mind?"

I didn't say anything.

"It's your dirty mind," said Vicki.

He said, "She's heard worse than that at Art College. A lot worse."

Emyr was peering closely at the card. "He's got an interesting-shaped head."

"It's like that joke that bald people tell," I said, taking it back. "About God creating human beings, and those heads that weren't perfect, He covered in hair."

"I don't know about that," said Vicki, laughing a little bit.

I said, "What is it about gay men? I don't know."

"Don't look at me," said Paul.

"They seem to keep all the best ones to themselves," I said to Vicki.

"Oh I don't know," she said. "Mine's not a bad catch. I'm not going to throw this one back, am I?" She stroked the downy hairs on her boyfriend's forearm.

"They all look the same these days," said Emyr, all bony shoulders, coffee froth making dirty brackets around his mouth. "Like clones, like robots. Have you noticed? So they can recognise each other I expect. There was a time not so long ago, they were trying to cover up how they looked, make it not so much a give-away, like. Pansies, my Mam used to call um. Then it was queers, wasn't it? Then it was gay."

"Now it's back to queers," I said. "Queer is OK. They like to be called queer."

"*Never*," said Emyr.

"Haven't you heard of Queer Power?" I said.

"Emyr hasn't even heard of Power Rangers," said Paul, with his hand on his girlfriend's bare knee, and they laughed.

"Hilarious, Paul," said Emyr. "You're such a wit, I'm not kidding, you ought to be on *Newsnight Review*."

"Yeah, there's a fair few shaved barnets on that," said Vicki. "They're all over the place nowadays, aren't they? You can't get away from them."

I looked at George Polish Name, on the card in my fingers. I don't know what attracts me to gay men, or gay women for that matter. Maybe I just feel safe with them. Maybe I don't feel threatened. With the shutters back and light falling on him, George is a beautiful object, his red ears sticking out, his bluish chin, his bony shoulders, the dot of white on his nipple ring, the three horizontal lines that segment his fat-free abdomen. The cupped, entwined fingers in his lap. I noticed as

I painted him for the first time that his hands seem much older than the rest of his body. They could be his father's hands.

"How do you find them? Models?" Emyr asked. He shot a glance at Paul. "Shut up. It's interesting, this."

Paul held up his hands, tucked in his chin.

I said, "I first saw George in The Fox. I thought, there's a really physical guy, but vulnerable, with shaved head and tattoos and who's done everything to himself to look mean, but with these warm eyes like a puppy. I felt like a man eyeing up some leggy blonde in a mini skirt. I couldn't take my eyes off of him. I wanted to know his name, where he lived, what he did for a living. Then I went up and said, Hi, my name's Stella Beatty, I'm a painter, will you sit for me please? Not quite those words, but something equally embarrassing, and George blushed. And from then on, I knew he was perfect. Pubs are great for models."

"You just went up to him? Just like that? And asked him?" said Emyr, astonished. "In a pub?"

"Yeah. Where else? I always used pubs and cafes in Edinburgh. I'm always looking for faces. Faces at bars, faces across a cafe, faces at a disco, anywhere."

"Isn't it embarrassing?"

I shook my head. "Not any more. I've gone past that point of thinking, oh shit. I pretend it's not me, it's this confident person I'm not. I just go up to them. I used to be shy, I'm quite a shy person really, but you can't afford to be. You have to say to yourself, you're a painter. It's your job. You have to find people to paint. It's as simple as that. You've got to earn a living. You see people. They attract you, for whatever reason...

"*Inspiration*," Emyr said, hunched over even more, eager beaver body language, hugging himself and grinning like there was something absurd and wonderful about the word.

"Are they real? The tattoos?" he said.

Paul was directing the packet of Silk Cut Extra Mild at his

girlfriend's mouth, like a microphone.

"People ask me if I make them up, if I just add them on. 'Course I don't, I mean, what's the point of that? I mean, the point is, that's the person, that's a part of them, that's why it's there."

She plucked a cigarette with her lips.

"And do you know a lot about the people you paint?" asked Emyr. "Do you know them really well, mostly?"

"When I'm painting I don't really want to know anything about them, they're an object. I'm not looking for information, or a story, like a Laughing Cavalier sort of thing, because that's too sentimental, too crass. Not that I'm not interested in them as people. I am, in the sense that I'm really interested in what makes people tick. I've always been interested in that. At school for instance, and always, even now, I always really notice hands, hands and heads. I can still picture exactly what my French teacher's hands looked like, more than I can remember anything she actually taught me: I could draw them now, the thick blue veins like paint from a tube, the big bulbs of these knuckles with arthritis."

Emyr said, "It must be amazing to have that kind of *observation*." It was another word he made a big dipper out of.

"I always used to watch, to stare, even on the bus down Princes Street, and wonder all these things about all these people. My mother would tell me off for being rude and showing her up. I could never understand why looking was such a crime. You know?"

Paul Rolt dragged the colour supplement onto his knee and resumed reading an article about Billie Piper.

"This is probably boring," I said.

"No," said Emyr. "It isn't. Not to me."

The others didn't say anything.

"At Art College, of course, they employed people for you to stare at," I said. "I don't know what my mother would have thought of that. But the models were terrible. Once I said to one of the tutors, I don't see why I should have to paint this Big Fat Old Man any more, I'm sick of it. And he said, Well, we can't get anybody else. As if, think yourself lucky for this Big Fat Old Git to draw. Then I read this thing in a book on David Hockey and he said that when he was at the Royal College he could not believe how *repulsive* some of the models were, and he complained, and they said, What's your problem? So I felt, right: there's David Hockney saying it, it's not just me."

Vicki was looking at her watch.

"Sorry," I said.

"Do you have any idea what a one-bedroom flat is going for in Bath?" she said. "Roughly?"

"No, not really."

Nobody said anything for a while.

"We've got our heart set on a honeymoon in Yucatan. I'm not quite sure where it is, but it's supposed to be beautiful."

"Mexico," said Paul, drawing a map of the Caribbean Sea in the air, livening up again.

"They have these little huts right on the beach," said Vicki. "Just like Robinson Crusoe. And these bars that serve cocktails and fruit, it just sounds like Paradise. It's expensive, but my attitude is, bugger it, you only go on honeymoon once, don't you?"

"Hopefully," I said.

"She made a mistake in the Seychelles," said Paul. "Tell her about your mistake in the Seychelles, Vic." Vicki looked blank. "You know." He make circles on his chest with his thumbs.

"Oh yeah," she said, covering her mouth. "I bought this beautiful bikini from Jolly's, in white, right? It looked beautiful on the beach, sunbathing, perfect."

"Then she went in the water."

"Then I went in the water and..." She made a startled face which was intended to convey everything, horror, embarrassment. She shook her head at the memory. "You know."

"She..."

"Don't!"

"Put it like this. There was not a lot left to the..."

"Paul, shut up!"

"Imagination, shall we say?"

She elbowed him. Her breasts shuddered slightly when she did. I noticed for the first time she was round-shouldered and not as petite as I first thought. She crossed her arms, but she wasn't embarrassed, not really. She was enjoying it. Her bloke kissed her and I watched moisture pass between their lips in the brief suction sound as stubble met freckles.

"Ah! What about that feller who puts half a dead cow in a tank then," said Vicki suddenly. "What do you think of *that*?"

"I think it's beautifully made," I said.

She groaned and so did her boyfriend. "I'm serious," I said. "Have you seen it?"

"No. Why would I want to see it?"

"Besides, what else would you do with a dead cow?"

"Eat it," she said. "That's what human beings are supposed to do with cows, isn't it? Eat them."

"McDonald's?" I said. "Burger King. Wimpy's."

"It's disgusting. A cow with a baby inside it. That's not Art, please don't tell me you think that's Art. What's so clever about sticking something like that in a glass tank?"

"Who says it has to be clever?"

Emyr said, "My Dad always said he'd never pay more than fifty quid for any work of art in the whole history of the world. Not a Rembrandt, not the Mona Lisa. Nothing."

"He'd pay fifty quid for a ticket to Cardiff Arms Park though, probably, wouldn't he?" said Paul.

"He didn't see the use," said Emyr.

The conversation seemed to last forever because they kept talking. Vicki kept tossing her hair from the back of her neck with both hands. She had these immaculate nails, these painted nails. She must have looked at the state of mine. You can't get it off, not even with Swarfega. She looked at me like I was a different species. Not exotic or interesting, just alien, like a vegetable on your plate you haven't encountered before.

So I tuned out quite a lot, and when I tuned back in, she was saying, "Of course I won't be available on Saturday and Sunday, but the best day for me is probably Wednesday when we have a half day, or Thursday between..." And the boyfriend had his Filofax out and he was full of, I'm doing this and I'm doing that, too. And the third one, I kept thinking, he's a possibility, but he was the one looking at his shoes, he was going, I will be available, sort of like twittering, and I thought No. No, none of you. *None of you* is any good.

But I kept smiling like an idiot. I think it was to cover up my real feelings, in case they showed through. I was such a coward. It was my fault. I should have said. Maybe I'd feel different now, if I'd just *said* there and then. Not that it would have made any difference to what happened. How could it?

And while they were going on about their availability, I wanted to stand up and say, stop, listen, none of you are any good to me, you're boring, you are all tedious shites and I can't bear sitting here any more – and it was so *pathetic* because what I ended up saying as I got up was, "Right, well, must dash. I didn't realise the time and, um – I'll give you all a ring next week." And I started to walk to the door.

"But you haven't got our phone numbers," Vicki piped up, a little startled but too dim to get it.

"Oh God. Have I not? Oh right!" I said, thinking I didn't want their poxy phone numbers, and before I know it there I am, writing it on the back of my hand, reading it back to them, checking it's correct.

Four

"She looked like somebody who should have been at home behind the counter at the Stroud and Swindon."

Gavin laughed at his forkful of lasagne. "That bad, eh?"

"Jesus! Worse," I said, knocking back the wine. "I'm not kidding. They were so boring, I don't know – I just glazed over, it was like *aeons*. I couldn't wait to get away and I had to sit there, sit there with the geek looking at his shoes and listen while she rattled on about her holidays and she'd say *what do you think of Picasso then*? Like, what the fuck? And, I'm not kidding, when she looked up and said *But you haven't got our phone number*! Jesus fucking Christ!..."

We laughed, tears bulging in our eyes, fanning the hot pasta in our mouths with our hands.

"You've got to phone them," Gavin said later. He'd seen the number written on my hand while we were in the kitchen cooking. He asked me if it was important. I'd started to rub it out with a wet finger and he'd stopped me. He said it again, now, as he criss-crossed his knife and fork on the empty plate. "Come on. You've got to phone them."

"Why?" I said, light headed from the second bottle of Andes Peak. "Bollocks."

"Go on, bollocks. It's not fair."

"It's not bloody fair being bloody boring-looking and wasting a morning of my time!"

"Go on." He got up and turned down the Morcheeba.

"Hey..." I said. "I was enjoying that."

"Go on. Do it now. Get it over with. You know if you don't, they're going to be ringing you up sooner or later."

I moaned. "I can't. Not now, I'm too pissed."

"Good." He took hold of both my hands and lifted me from my chair. "Do it, come on..."

"She was so boring."

"I know."

"She was so full of herself."

"I know. You said."

"They all were. So fucking *boring...*"

I started to laugh uncontrollably. Gavin laughed too. He hung loosely against the wall, his face falling against mine, lips to lips. I held his face. It was nice.

"I love you."

"You appreciate me now, then, eh?"

"No."

He read the number off my hand and dialled it, and held the receiver to the side of my head.

As the ringing tone burred, he slid his hand down the front of my trousers, behind my belt. I felt his fingertips in my pubic hair. I slapped his wrist. He kissed my ear, tugged it between his teeth. I smelled wine.

We laughed.

Vicki Hartwell answered the phone. There was music in the background.

I said, "Hello. This is Stella."

She said, "Stella! Great."

My heart dropped, so I said quickly, "Look, I'm awful sorry and everything, but I need a certain type. I'm doing this painting, and it's nothing to do with you, all of you -- but I'm only looking for certain faces. Sorry." The more I tried to embellish the thought, the worse it sounded. To me, anyway.

Her reaction was just an "Oh," as if she was completely surprised and didn't understand.

"It's not like you aren't pretty or anything," I added hastily, giggling. I had a headache now – a clash between sobering up and wanting to get hammered. I frowned.

She said, "I understand." And by now she sounded shirty a little bit.

I said, "I am sorry."

There was a gap. Somebody turned down the music. "Oh, well. It can't be helped." A tremor in the back of her throat now.

I started to get embarrassed. "I've got to go now," waiting for her reply, giving her a gap to speak in.

"Well thanks for ringing," she said. "Thanks for the coffee."

I hung up, and a moment later remembered that the coffees had been bought by her. It made me feel bad. I don't think she said it on purpose. I think that kind of guile was beyond her. She was upset. Perhaps.

Gavin had taken the plates into the kitchen and was dumping them in soapy water. I picke d up the salt and pepper from the table, and refuelled the two wine glasses.

She'd get over it. So would I.

Gavin came back and rubbed off the phone number on the back of my hand with a J-cloth.

"She loved herself," I said. "She loved herself too much."

"You're feeling guilty now," Gavin said.

"No."

"You're worried you hurt her feelings."

"No. She's too full of herself for that."

"Is that why you didn't like her then?"

"She was thick," I said. "She was thick as a plank and she was confident, with it. She thought she was the bee's knees. I like people with a bit of self doubt."

He puts his arms around me. "Is that why you like me?"

I said, "Who says I like you?"

We exchanged the wine breath in our mouths. He uncoiled my belt and unzipped my trousers. He stood behind me and pulled down my knickers and positioned his prick under my buttocks. It felt warm and gentle. His hands began massaging my shoulders as he stiffened harder and got bigger. I rubbed my cheek against his knuckles and whispered, "I like being naughty."

"You're my wife. I'm your husband. We can do what we like in our own home. Can't we?"

I said, "That's true." I took off my clothes, and then his, and we made love on the carpet, which felt uncomfortable, and great, and somehow criminal, and somehow good. He felt like what he was: a nice, good man. "I love you."

"Why's that?"

"Because you're big fat and ugly," I said.

Five

Vicki Hartwell. Vicki Hartwell.

I didn't even know her second name until I read the newspaper. The story first appeared on the Wednesday. The Wednesday after the Saturday.

Gavin came in with a Chronicle like he usually does on the way home from work. He'd been painting a Georgian ceiling up in the Circus and he went to lie in the bath. I was worried he'd done his back in again. He said he was in agony. I didn't see the early evening news, the ITV West news, it was probably on that. I just saw her face in the paper, on the front page, that blow up of her from her 18th birthday party, with a little bit of red-eye from the camera flash, and the teeth and the low cut blouse and a weeny bit squiffy, letting her hair down a bit and enjoying it.

I felt that woozy feeling you get when you stand on a cliff and lean over the edge and for a second it feels like nothing is holding you there. My first instinct was to call Gavin, but I just sat there, and didn't.

I said to myself, calm down, it's not so bad. It says MISSING. It doesn't say what's happened to her. It's not like they've found her body or anything, all chopped up. That's all it says, just MISSING.

I had to tell Gavin. I picked up the paper and went and tried the bathroom door.

It was locked. He always locks it. It always irritates me.

He said, "What?" Shirty.

"How long are you going to be?"

"Why?"

"Dinner's on the table in five minutes, that's why."

"All right. I'll be out in five minutes. OK?"

I went back to the table and sat with the paper spread out in front of me like a map. I closed it when I heard the bath plug pulled. Gavin prowled the room wrapped in a towel. "Where's the number for that chiropractor Jill was talking about?" I turned the paper over, face down. *Her* face down.

I looked in from the kitchen at him as I dished up the meal. He had a little wet curl on the back of his neck, as dark as Indian ink, head bent over the paper. We sat and ate. He didn't say I looked like I'd just seen a car accident or anything. He started at the back page, with the sports, flapping the paper in occasionally extravagant folds. Every mouthful of my food was forced in like a gag, stuffing words back down into me. I was waiting, and I knew what was coming, but I didn't know when. Then he said in a mumble: "Jesus. Did you read this?"

"What?" I said, butterflies inside.

"This girl..."

I said, "I know."

"Unbelievable... Right around the corner."

"Yes."

I thought, I'll tell him. I *will* tell him. How will I tell him? How?

"That night club, Manhattan's..."

"What do you think of the noodles?" I said. "I know it costs a bit more but you get better quality with the Marks stuff, don't you? That's what you pay for."

"She was born in Nailsea, where Roger comes from," said Gavin, surprised, and started to read it out: "Police worries intensified when they learned from Vicki's parents that the red-haired student at Bath University always let them know her plans in advance. She never went anywhere without picking up the phone, Mr Hartwell said, she knows what worriers we are and she's very responsible." He flickered a look at me, a shrug. "It seems to be entirely out of character, said DI Rob Kernow of Avon Constabulary, which gives us great cause for concern. If anybody has any clues as to Vicki's whereabouts please contact the nearest police station where all information will be treated in complete confidence." Another look. "In the early hours on Sunday morning a story of tragic misunderstandings quickly emerged. Vicki Hartwell had gone to the night club in Tilley Street on Saturday night in the company of her boyfriend Paul Rolt and his flatmate Emyr Winter. During the course of the evening Mr Rolt became annoyed that Vicki was spending time with some old school friends, and at 11.30 went home in a mini-cab from Ab Cabs in King's Square. Not knowing that Mr Rolt had gone home, Mr Winter also left Manhattan's to go to Skorpio's Kebab House in Millet Street with some student friends. Her schoolmates last saw Vicki at approximately 12.15, when she left the dance floor to look for her boyfriend. She has not been seen since.

"Vicki's photograph has been printed on a poster by the Chronicle and appears all along Tilley Street in the hope that it will jog somebody's memory. Police are asking for anyone with any information on Vicki to contact this CRIMESTOPPERS number, blah, blah..." Gavin's voice trailed off. He looked at his plate as if he'd forgotten that he'd eaten. He bent the paper in half and pushed it to me.

"I read it before. I told you." I got up. "Do you want a beer?"

"Have you got a cold one?"

"Think so."

He pulled the paper back, turned it back to him, picking his teeth. "Pretty girl, look, too..."

"Awful," I said in a small voice. "Awful..." I opened and closed drawers looking for a bottle opener.

"She'll turn up, Stell," Gavin said. "Don't get upset.

She'll probably turn up. They always do, one way or another..."

I brought him the beer.

"You're not having one?"

"No, I'm fine."

But I'm not thinking, I'm thinking of his words: *They always do, one way or another...*

One way or another...

Six

By the end of the week, the same picture was appearing in the nationals, bigger now, and it is saying things like POLICE FEAR FOR SAFETY OF VICKI. The police were still pleading for the public to come forward. It was all over the local TV news, Manhattan's in its tired neon scrawl, blinking, un-hip, corny, the police with their clipboards, talking to youngsters as they went into the disco the following Saturday night. Amish-tight WPCs contrasting with half-cut girlies, glittering-midriffed Pop Idol wannabes, biting their lips, arms crossed round their ribs as if trying to keep in their anorexic vital organs. Boyfriends loitering with their shirt tails out, tongues of their trainers lolling and cool and quietly hungry, thinking of their hair gel and not of the police's result that night, but theirs.

The mother was at the press conference, again, a repeat, looking like a ghost. I wondered, how can she go to the hairdresser's? How can she put on lipstick? How can she fill up the car with petrol? She looked frightened by the cameras, Delia Smith facing a firing squad. Her husband fussed over her hand like it was a precious object he had just found in the snow.

"What do you want for dinner?" I left the sofa-bed to Gavin with his long legs taking it over. "I've got the liver and bacon or the beef."

"I'm not fussed."

"They're both Not Suitable for Home Freezing, so we can have one tonight and the other one tomorrow night. What do you fancy?"

"They released the boyfriend, then."

"You're not listening to me."

"I'm watching the television."

"Bugger the television," I said. "Hello. I'm here, this is me. I'm real." It came out louder than I meant it to.

I went to the kitchen and he sloped after me. He hovered by the door while I unloaded the dishwasher.

"I keep thinking about her," he said, by way of explanation, opening and closing random cabinets. "Thinking she's out there somewhere, in a cellar. Some fucking nutter... Horrible, horrible..."

I looked at him hard. "You think I don't think about that?"

He looks hurt. Hurt that I look hurt. He doesn't understand anything. He takes the knife from me. "I'm cooking. I'll do it."

I take it back and puncture the film over the packets of liver and bacon. "I've started now. I'll do it." He goes back in and sits down.

Seven

I was at a dinner party when somebody said, "Is there any news about that girl who went missing? What was it? Four weeks ago?..."

"You think they'd turn up something," said the Welsh woman who'd already been racist about the Scots. "Fingertip search. Divers in the weir. Dogs. Helicopters, the lot. I mean, for someone to vanish without a trace, into thin air, virtually."

"Don't be stupid," said her husband. "It happens all the time." She looked momentarily crestfallen and her neck reddened as I watched her chasing some rocket and radicchio round the smear of balsamic vinegar on her plate.

"Dreadful," said the woman who came without a bottle. "Dreadful."

"What do you think happened?"

"Well it's obvious isn't it?" said her boyfriend, topping up his glass of red.

"Is it?" I said.

He looked mystified by my comment. He said, "Well. Some bloke, obviously."

Anna cleared the starter plates and told us that the main course would be a while, so we could feel free to pollute our lungs. We did. She was good like that, even though she'd given up for two years herself. She empathised with the addiction in others.

"What's her name?"

I listened to some wine pouring.

I said, "Vicki Hartwell." I wasn't sure if I said it out loud, so I heard myself say it a second time. "Vicki Hartwell."

"There are some nasty people in the world," said the woman who didn't bring a bottle.

"Her poor mother, that's what I keep thinking," said Gavin, clearing something from between his teeth with a fingernail. "What's the worst? Believing your daughter's dead or believing she's still alive?"

Anna came back into the room and announced, "Five minutes." She took off her apron and her husband rubbed her back and told her to relax.

"Alive," said the woman from the health food shop, stroking a roll-up. "Alive is worse. If it was me, if it was my daughter, I'd rather she was dead, anything, I'd rather they found the body. The idea of her *suffering...* you know?" She shivered under her hippy mane like she'd touched a snake. "God, I couldn't bear it. Not knowing. God. What you imagine is ten times worse."

I excused myself and went to the loo. I didn't need to go. I sat there in the minimal bathroom, no frilly toilet roll holder, no odd socks spilling from the laundry bin, no toothpaste stains around the sink. I considered if I could cry, and wash my face, and not look red-eyed when I returned to the table, or arouse attention, when there was a tap at the door. Gavin, asking if I was all right. Me, saying I am.

Eight

In the car driving home, Gavin said, "I don't know what's wrong with you. I was worried. It was embarrassing."

"Oh, it was embarrassing. Sorry." I turned down the heater. "Concentrate on the road. How much wine have you had?"

"One glass. Not even a glass, actually." He flipped the wipers to smear away specks of drizzle. "Is it something I've done? Tell me. Stella, is it me? What?"

I laughed through tight lips. It was supposed to mean, don't be ridiculous, but Gavin looked as though I'd mocked him, injured him. "No. It's not you." I rubbed my eyes. They felt like sandpaper.

By the time we got in, it was half past one. Still standing in my wet raincoat as he pulled out the sofa-bed, I said I was going to sleep in the bedroom. I said he had to be up early and my tossing and turning with my bad back kept him awake. I made it sound like I was thinking of him. He shrugged, plucking at the corners of the sheets. He said if I cared about him sleeping badly, I knew he always sleeps badly on his own. I said let's give it a crack. Just tonight. He said, "You're the boss."

I said, "No I'm not. Don't say that."

"What do you want me to say?"

That night I lay awake for ages, my eyes in a jetlagged daytime alertness out of synch with the sleeping world outside. Some time later I heard Gavin padding nakedly to the bathroom, I listened to the string pull light swinging and tapping against the wall, the extractor fan, the steady stream of piss, the flush kicking in finally on the third try. I heard him pause at the door, as the flush went into hissing mode, and he came into the darkened room and looked down at me. He stood beside the bed and whispered, "Stella? Are you all right?" I didn't move. I visualised his tall, naked body in the gloom, his square shoulders and collarbone catching a spill of light, his tousled pillow hair, his baby bewildered eyes. I listened to him breathing, half expecting him to get into bed beside me, or touch me with his warm workman's hands. My heart was beating hard. I kept my eyes tight shut, I played dead, and after a few more minutes, I heard the creaky boards counting his footsteps back to the sofa-bed.

Nine

The next morning he brought me breakfast in bed. He pampered me. Poached eggs on toast, done to perfection, runny, pot of tea, little milk jug, and a little chocolate valentine heart he must have got from the corner shop when he got the milk. He sat on the bed and kissed my cheek and said, "I've decided. I'm going to start decorating today. We're going to move back in here by the weekend. I'm sick of that bloody put-you-up. I'm going to chuck it out."

I don't know what it is with tea, whether it always tastes nicer when somebody else makes it. That tea was particularly nice.

By the time I'd got up he'd left, and I found another heart in red shiny paper Sellotaped to the corner of one of my canvases. I wanted to put it in a box, in cotton wool, in silk, like a diamond ring. I looked at the portrait I did of Gavin six months before, with the primary colours, the light bulb and the hula-hoop, propped against the wall. It caught something about him: the quizzical, cartoony optimism, the openness, the strength, the safety. He was a nicer person than I was. Than I could ever be.

I felt the pot and the tea was still warm enough to drink.

Ten

It's twelve weeks now. Three months.

The face I had no interest in is everywhere now, a mocking population explosion of clones shouting: VICKI HARTWELL - MISSING. Posters on walls, that grainy snapshot, bill-posted amongst the vivid pastels of the jungle and techno venues. In waiting rooms, at the doctor's surgery, in the pub. The face, the lipstick, the hair, the tipsy smile. I pass a shop window and I see it. I nip in a newsagent's and I see it. I buy a stamp at the Post Office and I see it. VICKI HARTWELL - MISSING.

She smiles at me in the hairdresser's salon from the poster with backward letters in my mirror.

"That girl. All this time. God. I wonder what's happened to her?" says my hairdresser, John. "Such an ordinary, attractive young girl, too..."

I say, "Do you think she's attractive?"

He shrugs and lowers his voice. "Well, I'd have got rid of that frizz for a start off. That went out with Pan's People, that did."

"She was to somebody," I say. "...Attractive, I mean."

"Oh yeah. Somebody must've fancied her, mustn't they? Somebody must've liked her face." He teases up some more random spikes. "You always think that stalkers are always after your Jill Dandos or your Mel Gibsons, but who knows what they fasten on to, really? Who knows what they're looking for? The hair, the eyes?" As he talks I look at Glamour and Elle on the coffee table with their panther-faced cover girls, ash-black faces and lilac, succulent lips, and waif-junkie child-bride fashion spreads, and think of the furious masturbators who use Freeman's catalogues, the baby clothes sections. Nothing is sacred, safe, any more. There's nothing that cannot be used. "Do you know why you fancy someone? I don't. It's a total mystery to me," he said, snipping.

Eleven

Six months, and she still hasn't been found.

"How did you do that? It's a humdinger." Gavin takes off his socks and boxer shorts and sits naked on the toilet seat. I look down into the Body Shop formaldehyde and see the dark cloud of a bruise on my thigh.

"I don't remember." I cup water over my breasts. "I didn't even notice I'd done it." I raise my knee out of the scum and examine it. It has a green penumbra and pointillist pricks of red in the centre. I sink it back under and consider the rest of me, like a pathologist might do. A gash on my forefinger from a pencil-sharpening scalpel. Dotted claw marks on the back of my hand from next door's cat. A scar from falling from a swing, aged six. Scabs, grazes with explanations lost in time. If I were dead, if they slid me out of a metal cabinet, what clues would there be?

Vicki Hartwell. Vicki Hartwell.

Repeat anything long enough and it becomes abstract, losing its meaning. It's no longer a name, just a mnemonic for a feeling, a feeling of dread. A dread of what's happened to her, of what might happen to us, any of us. Our bodies. What people might do to us. Can do to us. Cut us, bruise us, burn us, make us afraid, make us think we're going to die. How vulnerable we are. How easy it is for someone to do us pain if they want to.

"Can I get in after you? Is it still warm?"

He made circles in the water with his hand.

I sat up. Put on my specs. "I'm getting out."

"You don't have to."

"No, I've finished. You get in."

I stand up dripping, our naked bodies, one wet, one dry, passing each other without touching. I feel like, if he gets too close, he will know, by osmosis or something. It will seep out of my skin. I can see he thinks I'm being cold. He is right. I brush my teeth. I spit into the spiralling water, the minty froth flecked with blood from my gums. If I close my eyes I see her, her immaculate lipstick, playing with her shimmering hair, her manicured, slightly-chubby hand stroking her boyfriend's inner thigh.

"You've shaved your legs. Thanks for telling me." Gavin sinks into the formaldehyde. There's a nasty cut on my shin from the razor and I hope to God it'll heal.

Twelve

It is nine months since now she went missing, and the police are scaling down the investigation. The conclusion is that she either doesn't want to be found or something very bad has happened to her. The TV news shows the same footage of Manhattan's, a litany now, the shots as familiar as those of an endlessly repeated Tesco commercial. The detective in charge, DI Rob Kernow, looks older, as respectful as an undertaker, with the sound turned down on his life.

There isn't a day I don't think about her. I don't think there'll ever be a day now, when I don't think about Vicki Hartwell.

Gavin comes in from the pub. He's been drinking. I know what's coming and I dread the predictability. When we're in bed he presses his excruciatingly hot, erect penis against the side of my thigh and kisses my shoulder. I say, "Gavin." I feel him wilt and he turns away, and after a moment I turn and face his back. I try to detect some reaction in his breathing, but I can't. He says, "We've got to do something about this, Stella. If we don't it's the end. If sex goes out of a marriage it's the beginning of the end. We may as well say it's over, that's it." I say, "Is that what you feel, is that what you want?" I manage to sound as if I'm accusing him. He just sighs. Later that night I hear him lying on his back and I know he's wide awake and so am I. I can't bear to touch him. I daren't.

I think, it could be me in a ditch, in a coffin, in pieces, because I'm frightened, and it's killing me, it's killing us, if I let it.

Thirteen

The next morning I make him scrambled eggs on soda bread toast. He wakes groggy, still asleep when I put the tray on his knees and say, "I want to tell you something tonight. Something I should've told you a while ago and I have to tell you now.

He looks up, like I've told him he has six months to live. "Is it somebody else?"

"No, not in the way you think. Nothing like that."

"What is it then?"

"I'll meet you in the Fox."

"Is it bad?"

"It's nothing. Not really."

"It is something.

"It is something, to me, yes."

Fourteen

That lunchtime I get a phone call from my daughter up in Edinburgh. It's the usual voice that still sounds about twelve on the answerphone with a sing-song "Hi, Mum. Only me. Just wonderin' how you're doin'. I'm fine..." There's a reason for this call. I pick up. One of the paintings I did of her is propped against the wall. It turns out she's jacked it in with the creep she was besotted by. She got sick of handing him out her hard earned cash from the clothes shop and she's going to share a flat with Marje who makes sandwiches in a Deli off Princes Street. I say, "That's good news." She says, "Well..." It turns out she needs two hundred quid deposit. I can see it a mile off. I say I haven't got it, but by the end of the conversation she's saying "Thanks, Mum. How are things with you by the way?" I say, "Oh, the usual. Working hard." "And how's Gavin?" "He's working hard too." "Good, good."

Fifteen

I walk down Tilley Street past the police posters of Vicki Hartwell, past the burger take-away and Manhattan's, both gearing up for the Friday night throng, bouncers squeezed into bomber jackets like toothpaste in a tube, miming Tai Chi to each other.

The Fox is a builder's hang-out. I can never tell if the walls are tobacco-coloured paint or if it's the years of exhaled ale breath and tar. A blue cloud clings around the ceiling and the floor's already sticky. Gavin has commandeered a small table and a vodka has my name on it.

"Cheers."

The smoke is already biting the back of my throat so I think I might as well light up. He pushes a packet of cigarettes towards me. I look into his eyes. I light the last one in my old pack. "Thought I'd save you fighting your way to the cigarette machine," he says. "It's hootchin'."

I scan the bar. Old habits die hard. An arm like a tree-trunk is wrapped in tattoos like a malignant vine. A shaven-headed Vin Diesel lookalike kisses a girl on the cheek. An earring, a kit bag, straight from the gym. George Polish Name would fancy him. I like his head – soft, round like a baby's. My type. I remember seeing George here for the first time, soon after we moved down, not loud like his new builder mates, nothing to prove, no prejudice, no preconceptions, and admiring the Dennis the Menace badge on my leather jacket, drawing the other guys' attention to it, saying it was good, introducing me, saying it was fantastic, really meaning I was fantastic, showing me off to them, proud of me.

I say, "What did you do today?"

He wobbles his head unenthusiastically. "More shifting fireplaces. They're taking all those nice Victorian fireplaces out. God knows what they're doing with them. They're worth a fortune."

"Don't knock it. It's bringing in the money."

"I hate it."

"It'll be over at the end of the month."

"I still hate it."

"That's right," I say. "Make me feel guilty."

"How?" he says, pained. "Make you feel guilty? What have I said now? Christ's sake. I can't open my mouth any more."

I say, "Ask me about my day."

"Let me read your mind."

"Correct."

"Shitty."

"No. Productive."

"Oh. I never was good at reading minds." He doesn't ask me outright. Maybe doesn't want to know, maybe thinks whatever it is will go away. Is he making me suffer, or has he genuinely forgotten why we're here?

"I met that girl." I take a sip of vodka. "Vicki Hartwell."

I look up now. Gavin is colourless, as if someone has pulled the plug.

"She was that girl I told you about in the Metro Cafe. The one full of herself." My eyes wander off his face to the beer glass rings on the table. "I'm sorry, I'm really sorry. I know how you must feel, that I've been lying, deceiving, keeping something from you, but look, I was afraid. I thought you'd say go to the police. I couldn't face it. Then I felt a coward.

Then it just got out of hand, it was like if I kept it inside I could pretend it never happened, that I was never a part of it. But it felt worse and worse. It felt easier to forget about it than to face telling you. I know it was wrong. I just..." His eyes are focusing on arbitrary objects around the room, like he doesn't know where he is any more.

When I run out of words and he focuses on me, finally, it's like I'm a person who beat him as a child.

"Say something."

"What?"

"Anything. Please."

He stares at me, like he's seeing a person he's never seen before. "A girl's gone missing, Stella."

"I know, I know. What was I supposed to do? Tell the police? Tell them what? What could the police do? They've done everything. What difference would it make?"

"It doesn't matter, don't you see?"

I said, "I didn't do anything wrong. I didn't do anything to feel guilty about." The ashtray rattles as I poke the cigarette to death. Roy Orbison thunders from the juke box and a bunch of students throw up a cheer from a nearby table – whether for Roy or not I don't know.

Gavin says, "I'm going home." He's halfway to the door when he turns back. "Are you coming?" I don't move. He walks back to the table. "You're not walking home on your own. Are you coming?"

Sixteen

I go to the bathroom. It all pours out. There's no way he can't hear me, but he doesn't come to see what's wrong. I pull out yards of orange toilet roll and I'm sobbing and sniffling and by the time I look in the mirror my eyes and nostrils are red and raw and it feels like I've been pummelled in the stomach. I ache.

When I come back in, the TV is off and his clothes are folded on the armchair and he's in bed, naked, with his back to me. I undress and switch off the overhead light and get in, naked, ice cold.

It's impossible for me to sleep and neither can he. He isn't moving, but I can feel him, he's shifting around inside, unsettled and confused and raging but with nowhere to go. He's afraid even to move, that it'll betray something, or let something explode. I know how he feels. I kiss him on the chest, breathing out alcohol warmth onto his prickly hairs. I see a gulp go down his throat. He doesn't blink. I hear a couple of drunks outside singing the theme from *EastEnders*. The bed springs twang as I move closer and wrap one arm and one leg over him.

He says firmly, "For Christ's sake, Stella..."

A stone ball forms in my throat. I peel myself away from his body and lie rigidly on my back. His breathing breaks in little fits and starts, but he's trying to hide it. He's like a board lying next to me.

After an hour, perhaps two, I'm still wide awake. My eyes have got accustomed to the dark. It's hard even to shut them now, they're so dry and swollen and fixed. The room is grey, just monotone, colourless shapes with no people, no humanity, no life, no sound. I start to think I am the only person in this drowned, undreaming world, when I hear his disembodied voice, his croak say, "Why the fuck did you tell me?" It sounds like a stranger. It sounds like someone who despises me. "I didn't have to know this," it says, angry and lost, with his back still to me. "I didn't have to know."

Kid

Paul Finch

In London, I advise you not to look at signposts for the Victoria Line. And certainly never go down and use it, just in case the doors jam by accident and you're transported all the way to Baker's Wood. You see, I went to Baker's Wood... and I freely admit, it's the biggest mistake I ever made. I suppose I'd better give you the full details, so that you don't do the same stupid thing.

I was on my way to see my ex-wife at the time, to kick her fucking boyfriend's face in and tell her exactly what I thought of her. I went down to London in that heightened state for two reasons: firstly, because I was basically a thick northern lout, who was damned if any southern woofter was going to teach him about life; secondly, because I was up to the job – in fact, I was more than up to it. I'd been a tasty light-heavyweight at one time… I'd only been out of the game a year when this incident occurred, and at twenty-six, I was still as sharp as ever.

You won't recognise Baker's Wood on a map, because it isn't on any – I happened to know where it was because I'd been given directions by my ex-wife's unexpectedly compliant solicitor, who I suppose didn't want his face pushing in when I went to see him in his Liverpool office. I've never had much time for lawyers. They communally foster this 'elite-creature' image, someone who can say and do whatever he wants and then walk away from it; equally communally, they then hide their true personality behind it for the duration of their career. And rightly so, because in my experience, that true personality is someone you wouldn't want to know. The American term for a seedy lawyer – 'slimeball' – is well chosen. This one, who wore his bollocks on his sleeve when he was delivering in court, didn't even have to guts to lean out of his window and name-call after me until I was well down the street.

Not that it worried me. Broke, financially and in most other aspects of my life, I didn't care about anything. What was virtually my last fifty quid was spent on the one-way ticket south. As I alighted at Euston and made my way down to the Victoria, I felt only simmering rage. At that moment, the future didn't exist for me.

(And how true that was!)

But you know, things had once been great between me and Natalie. We'd married young, and for the right reasons, and when I'd first started making money we'd got round a bit, enjoying life any way we could. Her sharp tongue went with the beautiful brunette territory, I suppose, and I wasn't averse to slapping her down now and then, but on the whole things were okay. They only turned sour when I was banned from the ring.

I'd been in the best form of my life at the time: ten straight knock-outs and I was warming up for a shot at the European title. But health risks are high in boxing, especially at pro level. We all go into it with our eyes open, of course, but that doesn't lessen the danger. During one particularly brutal bout, I was sprayed with blood several times by my opposite number, and as I had more than a few nicks myself, the inevitable happened – I came down with a nasty case of hepatitis, which not only took me out of the game for a year but at one point almost killed me. Poundage dropped off my frame; before I knew what had happened, I was down from thirteen stone to ten.

Once I recovered, I worked like a dog to pump myself back up again, but I was impatient. Too impatient. "It'll come, Kid," Barney, our grouchy old trainer back at the Salford Lads Gym, used to assure me. "You're young enough, you're fit enough. Your body's like a Rolls Royce engine... everything you need's already there; all you've got to do is keep polishing it. Don't bugger about with the mechanism."

I wish I'd listened to him. I know now that I shouldn't have gone anywhere near steroids, but it's easy to be wise after the event. I got caught, of course, and my licence was revoked. A once promising career was over. Just like that. The Board understood my problem, but the bottom line was that I'd broken the law. The fight-game is an unsympathetic sport in that respect.

In archetypical washed-up boxer fashion, I then began to take things out on those I loved, i.e. Natalie. The slappings became smackings. She left me twice, though on both occasions she came back voluntarily, which is more than I deserved, being sunk in a mire of self-pity, drinking heavily and, because I'd developed a mild addiction to the steroids, spending money like it was going out of fashion and cultivating a psychopathic temper.

Soon the smackings became beatings. My wife was now putting up with more than any woman ever should. I was spoiling her lovely looks, making her life a living Hell. I went for counselling, but it was totally ineffective. I was still working out, you see, so as the addiction grew, so did my physical strength, my fury, my bitter conviction that everyone was to blame but me.

It came to a head during one night of unprecedented violence, when I put Natalie in hospital. I swear I didn't mean to hit her so hard, even in the midst of my rage, but I cracked her cheek-bone and knocked her out cold. And that wasn't the worst of it. She also lost the baby she hadn't dared tell me she was carrying. It was a miracle I wasn't arrested... but it later transpired she'd told them she'd slipped on the stairs. At the time I couldn't believe she'd spared me, and I wept with remorse when I went to visit her in hospital the next day. Natalie was cold with me, though. She simply said that she was filing for divorce. I assured her it would go through without a hitch. I still loved her, but I was no good for her. The only honourable thing to do, after years and years of in-your-face dishonour, was to step aside and let her get on with her life.

And then her fucking solicitor got involved.

The Scouse bastard ran rings round me. But then, when you're prepared to ruin people's lives and grind what's left of them into the dirt with your heel, as part of your daily job, you've an edge in ruthlessness that even street-toughs like me can't compete with.

Apparently, the amicable separation we'd agreed on was completely unacceptable. Those were his exact words in the letter he wrote to me, this fast-talking, sharp-suited man from Liverpool. "Completely unacceptable." First of all, there was the not inconsiderable matter of the house. Natalie was no longer living there by this time, but the mortgage was in both our names. If I wanted to stay there, I'd have to buy her out, and it wouldn't come cheap.

I agreed. What else could I do? It was all legal and above board.

Of course, our luxury four-bedroom villa in the suburbs was only one of the boxing nest-eggs I'd managed to tuck away, which Natalie had now allowed her smart lawyer to talk her into wanting. Next, and this was the straw that really broke the camel's back financially, because, as I said earlier, I had been spending dosh like there was no tomorrow, they wanted to discuss a settlement with regard to my assault on her... not to mention "other instances of cruelty". I read this second letter two or three times before it sank in that they were threatening to sue.

And just in case I got any ideas about contesting it, I was advised, I didn't have a leg to stand on; the moment he'd come on the case, Natalie's solicitor had amassed the necessary photographic and medical evidence. It was all packaged and ready to go. All I had to do was say "no". This in itself might have seemed reasonable – I had attacked her after all – but the sum they were demanding was ludicrous. I won't go into details but put it this way, you won't find a comparable figure in your telephone directory.

Hence my trip to Liverpool.

Hence my trip to London.

Hence... Baker's Wood.

Being a numbskull hooligan has its disadvantages. You fail to develop a sixth sense about impending danger, for example. I mean, I didn't know the capital very well in those days, but from the word go I should have realised there was something odd about Baker's Wood. To begin with, the tube station was all wrong. The platform was deserted and bare – there were no benches or bill-posters, no machines giving out bars of chocolate, no maps of the

Underground. At the top of the escalator, which, as far as I could see, ran only upwards, I slotted my ticket through the machine and passed out of the station via an exit that was more like a football ground turnstile, its revolving gate running from floor to ceiling. It was a narrow squeeze, and even though the mechanism was automated, it moved sluggishly, squealing in the process as if caked with rust.

From the outside, the station was a bleak, cinder-block affair. No windows were visible and the familiar logo was absent. But if that was strange, the neighbourhood was stranger still. It had the feel of an Ealing movie. The buildings were terraced brownstone tenements, squarish, flat-roofed, with railings at the front, steps leading up to the doors and fire-escapes in the alleys between them. Most looked the worse for wear, their uniform facades cracking or missing chunks of plaster. Here and there an entire building – or maybe even two – had vanished, the gap where it used to be filled with charred rubble; the stubs of metal beams and a few pieces of blackened wallpaper would be visible at either side. I wasn't entirely sure what these sites signified, but I had the bizarre idea they were bomb-damage. Of course, that was ridiculous. Wasn't it?

I glanced at the piece of paper I'd written Natalie's address on. She lived at 18 Cherry Tree Court. That wasn't a street-name I'd spotted yet. Not that I'd expected to. I suppose I should have bought myself a London A-Z, but in the way of all Brits 'abroad', I'd concentrated first on getting there, then planned to ask. That seemed like a good idea now. Across the road from me, I saw a man leaning on a lamp-post as if waiting for a bus, though from what I could see it wasn't a bus stop. I strolled across and, up close, found him a typical London slob. He wore a scruffy second-hand suit on a sparse, stooped frame. His face was thin, ferretty, unshaven, his eyes peevish and red-rimmed. Greasy grey hair straggled back to his collar.

"'Scuse me, mate," I said. "Looking for Cherry Tree Court. Can you point me the right way?"

He gave the barest shrug, hardly even glancing at me, and continued to lean on the street-light, his body-language registering total indifference. It was ignorant even by London standards. I was ready to walk away... I wanted to walk away, but unfortunately for this guy I'd been too ready for a fight from the outset.

"Cockney bastard!" I spat.

He looked round.

And I lamped him.

When I was a contender, one of the things that used to excite promoters about me was what they called my "thundering right hand". It certainly didn't let me down on this occasion. The scumbag fell in a heap, like he'd been neck-shot or something. His eyes rolled white before he hit the flagstones.

The road was clear, so I crossed back over, idly. On the far pavement, I noticed a face looking down at me through a dusty groundfloor window. It was the face of a woman – pudgy, sallow, with lank hair hanging in strings. She must have seen what had happened, but didn't seem the least concerned. She was staring at me in a vague, uninterested sort of way, as if there was nothing else to stare at. I glanced back across the street. The man was still lying unconscious, and to my amazement, another man – an older man, bent and shabby – slouched past, hands in pockets. He never even glanced at the prone figure.

I was stung. I knew that Londoners were way down the list in the friendliness league, but this was something else. It made me feel even better about the mission I was on. Maybe I'd thump a few more before I went home again.

Apparently, though, I wasn't the only one with violence in mind. I wandered the next street and came to an area of parkland – I say 'parkland', but it was more like a mini-jungle. The paths were weedy and untended, the grass and bushes thickly overgrown and hung with litter. On a bench half way across, I saw a white-haired woman in an overcoat. She was nodding to herself, and making odd 'clucking' noises. She was also drinking from a bottle of meths. As I approached her, two figures suddenly appeared on the path at the far end. They were policemen, walking side by side in that relaxed way. They'd be the obvious people to ask for directions, but what if they started to ask questions of their own? What if someone had already reported the assault in the next street?

I backed away into the undergrowth to let them pass, watching as they advanced. Despite the fact that it was now early summer, and a warm one at that, neither of them wore the short-sleeved white shirts so familiar on London bobbies. They were in heavy overcoats, and instead of helmets, flat hats, in the style of the police in my home town, Manchester. Fleetingly, I wondered if they were specials. Either way, they stopped and began to speak to the drunken woman. A few easy words were exchanged, though the woman's speech, as before, consisted mainly of clucks and titters.

Then, suddenly, something happened.

As casually as you like, one of the two officers drew his truncheon – an old-fashioned thing, long, nobbled, fashioned from blackthorn or something – and smacked her across the head with it. Not once, not twice, but three times. The first blow probably knocked her unconscious, if it didn't kill her; the other two were added for good measure.

My spine went cold. The woman slumped sideways onto the bench, her floppy white curls slowly reddening. The second policeman reached down, took the meths from her twitching hand and treated himself to a gulp, before passing it on to his partner. Side by side, chatting, they proceeded along the footpath, the bottle moving between them until it was empty, when it was carelessly tossed away.

I'd seen enough, and fought my way out through the undergrowth, sprinting down the first street I came to. The police I was used to – the Salford division in Greater Manchester – were notoriously tough. Even now, in the caring 21st Century, they kept on top of my home town's criminal population through brute force, but I had never seen anything like that: the fact that it was so unnecessary, the fact that it had been done in public and at the same time so casually, as if there was no danger anyone would see, or if they did, there was no danger they'd report. In addition, of course, there was the fact that it had happened at all. It's no cliche; in Britain, policemen do not do things like that. Acts of rash, unprovoked violence are the preserve of twisted individuals like me. What the hell was this?

When I reached the end of the next block, I was hopelessly lost. I looked around wildly, no longer quite sure what I was going to say to Natalie when, or if, I tracked her down. I suppose it was ironic: I myself had just flattened a guy for virtually nothing, then, no more than a couple of minutes later, I'd been terrified by seeing someone else do exactly the same thing. There was a lesson to be learned there somewhere, but at that moment I didn't have time for it.

I had to find Cherry Tree Court, and quickly. But for the first time I now felt I was seeing Baker's Wood properly. It wasn't so much underprivileged, as derelict. Everywhere I looked, windows were cracked or boarded over. What few front gardens there were, were a profusion of weeds and thorns. The cracks riddling the pavements were thick with greenery. Drain-pipes had fallen down, bins had been overturned. And then there were the people. Such people... drab, lifeless figures, shuffling along at a snail's pace, hanging around in doorways or sitting on steps, gazing at nothing. The few cars I'd seen were rusted wrecks. No traffic of any description was visible. A bigger mystery still was what Natalie was doing here. The guy she'd moved in with was apparently some whizz-kid she'd known from her youth. He was supposed to be in computer-sales; surely he could afford better than this?

I was just trying to make sense of it, when I spied the words 'Cherry Tree Court'. They were on a rusted name-plate, hanging from the gable-wall of a nearby building. Bewildered, I approached it, then made my way up the steps and entered its lobby. The first thing I encountered inside was loose floorboarding, littered with trash. Cockroaches skittered back and forth in front of me. This was straight back to my childhood and the slum-tenement orphanage where I'd been raised by hard-handed Irish nuns. I couldn't imagine Natalie putting up with this.

Flat 18 was on the second floor, at the top of a steep, rickety stair. The door was unlocked, and when I opened it, I found something akin to closet-space. It was a bed-sit and no more, with neither sink nor toilet, and one narrow, broken window with a ragged drape over it. The carpet was threadbare, the bed little more than an iron frame with a thin mattress on top. Above my head, strips of damp paper hung down fom a water-marked ceiling.

After the things I'd seen outside, I wasn't surprised. Neither was I surprised that it was empty. What did surprise me was the sight of money. It was on the bed in a neat pile; four old-fashioned one-pound notes, frayed and dog-eared, and two fifty-pence pieces, tarnished by age. There was also a folded note. When I opened it, I found that it was addressed to me. Not by name, I hasten to add, but addressed to me all the same:

Resident

This is your bi-monthly allowance. Spend it well. There won't be anything else until August.

It had been type-written, and looked like the photo-copy of a photo-copy of a photo-copy...

When I put it down, there was chill sweat on my brow. My heart was suddenly battering my rib-cage. I held my ground for a moment, a terrible panic threatening to overwhelm me, then turned to flee. But no sooner had I left the door than I saw two familiar figures coming up the stairs towards me, side by side, completely blocking my way.

I stopped in my tracks.

It was the two policemen from the park, but from this range it was plain that some kind of deception was going on. Their hair was coiling and greasy and far too long for real constables – it hung down to their shoulders. They were unshaven and brutish, their broad grins showing rotted and broken teeth. The uniforms they wore – the overcoats and flat-hats – were makeshift rent-a-cop outfits. The right colour, but that was about all; they weren't even in good nick, showing rips and dirt. Both men were tall, and as broad as apes. More to the point, they were brandishing their truncheons, and there was no doubt those were real.

"Welcome to Baker's Wood," one of them said, in nasal Brummie. "The entrance fee's whatever you've got in your pockets, plus your first two months' allowance."

The other one chuckled.

"What entrance fee?" I said. "What's going on?"

They were now right in front of me, the stench of methylated spirits sickening. The first one was no longer smiling. His lips curled into a scowl, and he prodded me sharply with his baton. "You're not here to ask questions, mate. You're here to do as you're fucking told!"

"Where... where's here?" I asked, in my best nervous-newcomer voice.

"Dumbest fucking cluck, yet," the bloke replied, shaking his head and glancing round at his mate.

And in that split-second, I threw the right hand. Tough as he looked, I doubt he'd ever been hit harder. He catapulted backwards, slamming into the wall. The other one took a wild swipe at me, but I dodged it easily, then got in four quick shots, two to his body, two to his head. He went down in a heap, his mouth brimming with blood.

Seconds later I was out on the street, running wildly in the direction of the tube station. One part of Baker's Wood looks the same as another, however, and soon I was going in circles, charging up and down the same alleys, racing back and forth across the same streets. Even then, the lethargic locals showed little interest in me... until I finally grabbed one by the collar of his string-vest and threatened to smash his face to pulp.

He was a toothless oldie, visibly petrified, but when I demanded to know which way the Underground station lay, he looked perplexed. "What... what do you want to go there for?" he stammered.

"Just tell me, or I'll beat your head like a drum!"

With shaking finger, he pointed. "Keep... keep going. You can't miss it."

I threw him down and hared off. The street took me past Cherry Tree Court again, from the inside of which I could now hear shouting and swearing. I continued running, and a moment later heard the angry blast of an old-fashioned police-whistle. I didn't look back, but nipped around the next corner I came to, and there, directly before me, was the station. I dashed up to it, but only when I got there, did it strike me that there was no entrance. The turnstile I'd come out through was exit-only; it simply locked when I tried to push it backwards. Frustrated, I ran right around the building, kicking through all sorts of rubble but failing to find another door.

I stood there, bewildered and panting, only for another whistle-blast and renewed shouting to come echoing up the street towards me. I could now hear large numbers of voices – it sounded like a mob. I remembered the old horror movies I'd seen, when East End crowds would come out en masse to track down Mr. Hyde or Jack the Ripper. Once again, I ran.

A minute later, I came to a shop. It was on a tight corner, only metal grilles and dried newspaper covering its windows. I rushed in through the open door, finding myself in dank shadows, surrounded by heaped empty boxes. A half-melted candle and a few scraps of vegetables were visible on a low counter. From a rocking-chair behind it, a slatternly woman with a lit cigar watched me curiously. It was the sort of scene you'd expect in Communist Romania or some such place, where the economy has totally failed but one or two are just scraping along by exploiting the rest.

I tried to smile at her, but sweat trickled down my nose. Then we heard the hue-and-cry out in the street, and the woman's eyes widened. With surprising agility, she leaped up, scrambled round from behind the counter and before I could say "bitch", had dashed outside, crying at the top of her raucous Cockney voice:

"In 'ere! 'Ee's in 'ere!"

Cursing, I chased her out, shoved her violently over, then hurtled away down the next ginnel, leaping over bins and dozing vagrants. At the far end of it, there was a moment of joy, followed promptly by a stunning disappointment.

Right in front of me there was an old street-sign: rusted in patches and hanging at an angle on its post, but it was a sign I recognised. It read 'Pimlico 2', and had an arrow pointing to the right. This was altogether more promising, and I ran on, finding myself on a high street of some sort, still devoid of traffic, but wider than any of the others, with the gutted shells of shops running in unbroken lines down either flank. One or two were still in operation, their ragged keepers loafing in the doorways. I ignored them as I dashed past.

The ranting mob was close behind, but I was almost free. It didn't matter how damaged this hick backwater I'd stumbled into was, this forgotten corner of the city… the rest of London was close at hand. I fancied I could hear the grumbling of red buses and black cabs. I ran all the harder, blood pounding in my ears. Pimlico was only two miles. And I wouldn't even need a passport – I hooted with laughter.

I'd easily outrun them, I told myself. I was still an athlete. I glanced back once, a jeering expression on my sweating face. There wasn't even a sign of pursuit, though I glanced round again and again as I pelted along, just to be sure. Which meant that I wasn't watching where I was going…

Thankfully, the stench hit me before the wall did.

I came to a staggering halt, one hand clapped to my nose and mouth. A vile fetor filled the air – bitter-sweet, but stale as vomit. I backed unsteadily away from the four objects lying on the road, bluebottles swarming off them. Human corpses... in varying stages of decay. That wasn't the only shock. Several yards behind them, filling the road from one side to the other and towering over me to the tune of eighteen feet was a sheer brick-wall.

I gaped up at it. Without doubt it shouldn't be here. This street was a key artery of the district – you could tell that just by looking at it. Yet all of a sudden it ran headlong into this thing? This thing which had no gate in it, no portal of any visible sort. My eyes followed it across the road, from one side to the other. At either end, it adjoined the buildings with heavy brick buttresses.

It wasn't just a wall, I realised. It was a fortification; a rampart built to withstand a siege... in this case, a siege from within.

I glanced down at the bodies again. A couple were skeletons in rags. The others were more recent; yellow and emaciated, cracking open, riddled with maggots, stinking beyond belief. Holes had been ripped through them. What looked like smears of blackened blood were visible on the road-surface.

Memories of a hundred old-time POW movies flashed through my mind... about what you could expect if you approached the wire. Almost without thinking, I picked up a hunk of plaster and tossed it towards the wall. At once, there was an explosion of automatic gunfire, and the projectile was shattered to fragments in mid-air.

I jumped back, glancing wildly right to left, but seeing only broken-down doors, and the empty eyes of burned-out shops. Dismayed, I fled down a side-alley to the next street, but found the same thing – another high wall, more rotted cadavers strewing its feet. The next road was the same, and the one after that. And yet, all the time, from the other side, I could hear the crash and roar of London traffic. I wanted to yank out my hair as I stood there in the smoke and heat and dust of the summer evening, unable even to approach let alone try to climb.

I cast another stone, but again some hidden gunner shot it to atoms with chilling accuracy. And then there were voices. I turned.

A chugging old pick-up truck had pulled into the cul-de-sac behind me. From what I could see, it was on its last legs – rusted to the bones, filthy, pouring out pollution. Ten or eleven of the phoney cops were in the back of it, all armed with staves. Following behind, at a safe distance, was a mob of locals. They too were carrying weapons: bats, pipes, belts, knives. They approached me warily, eventually coming to a halt. When the cops jumped down from the van, they formed a skirmish line and slowly advanced. My back was to the wall… literally. I had no option but to go forward.

What then followed was a whirlwind of violence even by the standards I was used to. I threw punch after punch, making as many tell as possible. Soon my knuckles were torn and bleeding. Phoney cops lay in heaps around me. But their numbers were overwhelming, especially when the civilian mob joined in on their side. Blows rained down, hands grabbed at me. Through red-frothed lips, I shrieked that I could take anything they threw, that my jaw was cast-iron. I lashed this way and that, yet no matter how many I knocked down there were always more to take their place.

Eventually I was forced to my knees, my arms seized and restrained. Battered and bruised, I was yanked back to my feet and frog-marched to the rear of the pick-up truck, where handcuffs – attached by a chain to the rear bumper – were snapped to my wrists. Jeering and spitting, the crowd allowed themselves to be ushered back, and the two coppers I'd punched out earlier came forward. I'm glad to say they were both nursing severely broken faces. One was still bleeding profusely from his nose and eyebrow. The other's mouth looked like raw beefsteak – I think I'd knocked out his entire top row of teeth. They stared at me with bleak hatred, but I was still too stupefied with shock at what was going on to really prepare for what happened next.

They leathered me.

With their truncheons.

And I mean *leathered.*

Primarily it was my back and buttocks, but in all my prize-fights I'd never taken such punishment. I don't know how long it lasted, but I sank down in a faint at least twice, wracked with nauseating pain.

The next thing I knew, the van was moving slowly and I was being dragged along on my knees. I tried to get to my feet but was too numb to do more than stumble drunkenly along, and fell frequently. They were parading me through their streets, I realised. People herded out to stand on the pavements, mocking and cat-calling. Some came forward to punch or kick me. Others contended themselves with throwing rubbish. It was a nightmare.

I didn't know where they intended to take me... possibly some grim police station, where I'd be thrown into a squalid cell for more brutality to come. Even stupoured as I was, I'd come to realise that whatever this place was, it was no part of the England I remembered. For all I knew, they could be taking me to a chopping-block or a stake with faggots piled around it. Neither option would have surprised me… so imagine how stunned I was when they actually took me home.

Home, of course, was that rat-hole of a flat back at Cherry Tree Court. They unfastened my handcuffs, hauled me up the stairs and flung me into that dingy little room without ceremony. The door banged closed and they were gone.

It was a wretched place – drab, dirty – but as I fell onto that thin mattress, for all its horsehair poking out and its loose springs, I was too weak and exhausted to think of anything but sleep.

The next morning, I was hungry, headachey and bathed in sticky sweat. I was also stiff as an ironing-board. Every joint was bruised. When I sat up, it was like a corroded statue trying to creak into life. I fell back and lay there, helpless, endlessly mulling over the events of the previous day. If it wasn't for the dank ceiling above me, and the skittering of roaches along the skirting boards, I'd have fancied it some delirious dream.

I couldn't stay there forever, of course. My stomach felt like it was digesting itself, and I was gasping for a drink of water. Agonised, I lurched up and scanned the dim room for the money they'd left me. It was now missing. What was it those two bastards had said – entrance fee? I shook my head at my naivety. In the immortal words of a famous old comic, there was a thief in this prison.

Minutes passed as I considered my position. I was determined that I wasn't staying. They could throw up as many walls as they wanted, recruit as many thugs as they could find to guard it, but they weren't keeping *me*! First of all, though, I had to take stock of my surroundings. Real stock. I needed a proper overview.

I limped out of the room, and saw that the stairway led past my flat up to higher floors. I followed it and eventually emerged into muggy, cloudy sunlight. I was on the roof. Some time in the past it had been tarred, but much of that was now worn away and bare rotten lathes were visible, which I was careful not to step on. In the very middle, something that looked like a giant rabbit-hutch – a haphazard construction of planks, knocked together amateurishly and now streaked with black-grey birdshit. One entire wall was composed of wire-netting, much of it loose.

I approached the thin g, baffled. A man was inside it... an old man, slightly stooped and with long white hair. His shrunken frame was clad with in indescribably filthy pyjamas. He was seated on a three-legged stool, holding a scrawny bundle of feathers which I recognised as a sparrow, and grooming it with a long, nicotine-brown finger. Various other birds were perched around him, either on his shoulders, or on clothes-pegs hammered between the planks to serve as perches. At my approach, they set up a wild fluttering, exiting the hutch via an aperture at the back. Only the one he was clutching remained where it was, cheeping contentedly.

"I watched you yesterday," the man said, without looking up. "Impressive effort. Futile, but impressive."

"Who are you?" I asked him.

He glanced idly round. His cheekbones were knife-blades in crinkled sacking, his eyes dull grey marbles. Folds of empty flesh hung from his throat. "No-one," he replied. His voice was croaky, his accent vaguely Cockney. "Your neighbour, I suppose. If that means anything. I'm in seventeen."

At least this one was sane, I thought. I approached the wire. "I'm looking for my ex-wife."

"Hope you find her." He continued grooming his bird.

"She was in eighteen before me," I added. "Natalie. Natalie Driscoll."

He seemed indifferent. "I never ask any names."

"Maybe you saw her then? Dark brown hair, longish. Italian-looking. Very pretty."

He shrugged. "Maybe."

"What does 'maybe' mean?" I found myself growing irritated again.

"It means maybe. It means I'm not sure. I don't know... take your pick."

"You're not very helpful."

He smiled to himself. "I'm not here to be helpful."

"What exactly are you here for?"

He sniffed, giving it some thought. "Burglary, I suppose. Shop-lifting. That sort of thing."

"So you're being punished?"

He blinked at me, surprised that I'd even asked such a question. "We all are."

"You stood trial?" I asked.

"Did you?"

He didn't even look at me. He knew what my answer would be.

I turned and surveyed the district. The rookeries of Baker's Wood were spread out on all sides; more flat roofs, more broken windows, more fire-escapes. Deep canyons ran between them, smoky, hazy with summer heat. From this vantage point, the perimeter was visible – high walls blocked off the main thoroughfares. Beyond them, a grey stubble of indistinct images swam in oily smog; buildings with straight edges and clean facades, I thought – cranes, moving vehicles, sunlight glinting on their chrome bumpers. Were those four towers I could see the smoke-stacks of Battersea Power Station?

"This is just impossible," I said slowly. "It can't happen. It can't!"

The man opened his hands and the bird flew away. "Bloody sparrows," he said. "They'll never make carrier-pigeons. One of these days I'll give up."

I rounded on him. "Could they have used my wife to lure me here?"

The man rose from his stool. “It was a missing sister in my case.” He shuffled out through the door. “They told me a loan-shark I owed money to had nabbed her and brought her down here for safe-keeping.”

I stuck a thumb over my shoulder. “Those walls aren’t unclimable, you know.”

He seemed almost amused. “But they are well-defended. I thought you’d found that out for yourself.”

I shrugged. “It’s only a matter of finding the snipers.”

He shook his head. “Or the swivel-mounted machine-pistols with the armour-piercing bullets and laser beam triggers.”

I gazed at him for a moment, then looked back towards the perimeter. Armour-piercing, lasers? It would certainly explain the hair-trigger response, the uncanny accuracy.

“Not that I understand what any of that means, of course,” the bird man added. “But I keep my ears open.”

I walked to the edge of the roof and peered down. Fifty feet below, there were figures in the street. Some were moving, but only laboriously, as if intolerably burdened. Most were lounging about, sitting on steps, leaning by lamp posts... watching the dry and dusty day go by. Their vegetable-like inactivity was chilling. In fact it was more than chilling. It was hideous, appalling, completely inhuman. They were like things without brains, zombies almost. And this cryptic, cynical creature from the pigeon coop was typical of them.

I turned back to him. “Surely somebody’s tried to escape?”

He made an impassive gesture. “People think about escape. But there are no really hardened criminals here. No gangsters, no murderers, no bank-robbers... better to keep them in the real prisons, where they can be watched.” He gave a seedy, almost leering grin. “No, we’re the sneak-thieves, the drunks, the spivs... the wife-beaters maybe.”

I looked at him sharply.

“We’re the nuisance value,” he went on. “The ones they’d rather not spend money on. The ones they can sweep under the carpet and forget, because in the unlikely event anyone should notice we're missing, they wouldn't worry enough about it to ask."

He scratched the side of his nose, and sniffed again, as if bored.

"And that's your final assessment, is it?" I said. "We're here, and there's no other outcome? Christ... you people are pathetic."

"You're entitled to your opinion, of course. Maybe you'll have a different one when you've been here as long as I have."

"And how long is that?" This, I supposed, was the million-dollar question.

He cast his mind back. "When was it... oh, autumn, 19... 1951."

For a moment I thought I'd misheard. "1951?"

He nodded. "Place hadn't been open for business too long then... but parts of the city had been designated unsafe for habitation, owing to the bombing. All sealed off, they were. Then there was the government mentality… they'd got used to the idea of concentration camps, you see. Seemed like a good idea, I suppose. They needed a fresh start, after all. Felt they had to get rid of the rabble."

Incredibly, he winked at me. Then he cackled. "You must admit, it worked for a while. They do tell me the '50s was far and away the happiest time to be living in Britain."

"You're mad," I said, taking a step away from him.

He rambled on: "'Course... '60s, '70s come along, '80s, '90s. Yobbo population's on the increase again. Even overwhelms this system."

"Stark, raving mad!"

He fixed me with his loopy grin. "Not as if they can just let us all go, though, is it!"

I fled from him.

"They can't never do that!" he shouted after me.

I all but flew down the rickety stairway. 1951! 195-bloody-1! He had to be kidding! He had to be! But he wasn't... I could feel it in my bones. He bloody-well wasn't!

I emerged onto the street in a panic-stricken stagger. For seconds I ran in circles, lurching this way and that, temporarily unhinged. I threw my mind back to 1951: Elvis... no, even bloody Elvis wasn't around in those days! The Korean War was on, though. The first hydrogen bombs, the Festival of Britain! Jesus H. Christ, it was like half a century ago, and that crazy old codger had been in here all that time... *because he was a nuisance.*

I charged down the first street I came to. I had to get out. I had to. I had this vague idea I'd just scale the perimeter wall, ducking and dodging the bullets. Of course, by the time I came within sight of one, common sense had re-asserted itself. I slowed to a walk as I approached, breathing hard. Swivel-mounted machine-pistols, laser-triggers...

I stopped in my tracks, knowing it was futile. The wall lowered across my vision, an impassable barrier. As before, sounds of city life came from the other side.

I wondered what exactly was over there; what it looked like from the outside. The facade of a derelict warehouse, maybe? A row of permanently condemned terraced-houses? How about an office block... one of those nobody ever sees open for business? Then again, why disguise it? We've all seen them before, probably in our own towns. Narrow streets which suddenly end in a high, faceless wall. A wall no-one questions, no-one wonders about. A wall which might as well not even be there.

Towns are all about walls. We're so used to them that we don't really see them, let alone stop to ask what's on the other side. We simply accept walls. And there, I think, was the secret.

That night, in the poky hole that had become my home, I baked. June can be merciless in the inner city. I lay on the mattress, sweltering. Everything around me was damp and mildewed, the ragged curtains hung still, there was a rank stench in the air. It made me brood all the more on the chances of escape. The walls were out, it seemed; the subway station was out! And then, something occurred to me… I sat up.

This hellish prison, this Warsaw Ghetto policed so effectively by its own inmates, gave the impression that all who entered, remained; that once you were in, there was no way out. Yet that had to be a fallacy, because the supplies arrived from somewhere. No matter that they were the scrapings of someone's plate, they still had to be delivered. Someone had to bring them in.

It was a chance in a hundred, but at least it was a chance. A surge of energy went through me. I almost laughed. They'd have to try harder than this if they wanted to keep a grip on me.

The following day I went to a shop on the corner. Corrugated metal covered the windows, but the front door was open. Inside, it was a stuffy, airless oven. Junk of every description was heaped there, but the shelves behind the counter were empty. I banged on the woodwork impatiently and a man appeared from the back room. He was like something from Dickens: short, wizened, wearing a long silk dressing-gown and, ridiculously, a fez. Lank ginger hair fringed his crinkled, nut-like face. "I've no bread, I've no meat!" he said immediately. "'Taters is all. Maybe a carrot or two, if I can dig 'em up."

I feigned disappointment. "When will you next have something in?"

"Tomorrow," he replied. "No sooner. Now... what can I do you for?"

I grinned at him. "Nothing. Ta. You've done enough."

I vacated the shop, leaving him staring after me, puzzled.

At the end of the street, I secreted myself into a burned-out doorway. Things couldn't have been better. If the old bastard expected to be restocked by tomorrow, he had to be collecting his supplies some time today. It was just a matter of keeping tabs on him. So I waited, and I watched the shop. It was highly possible, of course, that he would leave the premises by the rear, but that didn't worry me too much. I doubted he'd leave the place open.

I had to wait most of the day, getting hungrier and thirstier. Come early evening, though, with the sun still high and intensely hot, he suddenly emerged with an empty sack on his shoulder. He drew a shutter on the door, fastened it with a padlock and set off in furtive manner, looking for all the world like Fagin on his way to meet Sykes. I followed at a discreet distance.

We traversed several streets, and at last came to a semi-derelict tenement standing alone on waste ground. The shopkeeper glanced round once, missing me completely as I hunkered down behind a dustbin, then, slowly and with much wheezing, ascended to the roof by a fire-escape. I gazed after him, perplexed. I'd expected him to lead me to some secret aperture in one of the outer walls.

I kept a careful watch on the building for the next hour or so, kicking my feet, shuffling back and forth as if passing the time of day. Several more of the local traders arrived – typical London marketeers and wideboys, in aprons and pork pie hats. Some even had their hair greased back and wore jewelry, keeping up a juvenile pretence of their old showy lifestyles. One by one they climbed to the roof, and I held my ground, none the wiser.

Another hour passed, and only then, when a sudden black dot appeared on the setting sun, and a distant *whirr* of rotor-blades cut through the still of the evening, did the truth strike home – a helicopter drop. Excitement gripped me, though such a development was less than I'd hoped for. It wouldn't be easy stowing away on a chopper, but what option did I have?

I hurtled up the iron stairway, my feet clanking on the treads, no longer caring that I might be heard or spotted. Escape was the only thing that mattered. I couldn't be held; I wouldn't be.

The traders were gathered on the roof in a wide semi-circle. One of the phoney cops was on duty with them, truncheon drawn, though he seemed bored with the whole affair... too bored to notice my arrival. I sidled in among them with less difficulty than I'd expected, and a few moments later, the chopper was above us, a huge-bellied beast of black metal, bearing no distinguishing marks.

It descended to about ten feet, but there began to hover, and instead of putting down, lowered nets filled with supplies: cardboard boxes, bulging sacks, heavy parcels made from newspaper and string. As they hit the deck, most of them burst or fell over, spilling potatoes and carrots, loaves of bread, apples and bananas, tinned foods, cartons of milk, bottles of water, packets of sausages or bacon, even a few boxes of cigs and a case or two of beer.

The traders moved forward in a wave. There was no queuing, no discussion, no orderly distribution; it was a scrum, pure and simple. They fought for whatever they could get their hands on. In the resulting chaos, I went unnoticed. As far as I could see, the only way out of this was via the now empty-netting. It was highly likely someone would notice me then, but it was a risk I'd have to take... there didn't look as if there was any communication with the pilot.

I waited with baited breath as the brawl went on. The vast bulk of the supplies were now scattered over the roof-top, and the traders were capering among them, shoving things into sacks and bags. I began to edge forward. Still, no-one had spotted me. And why should they? Even the cop, I noticed, was claiming his share. He'd already stuffed two or three packets of fags into his pockets, and was now wrestling with another man over a dusty four-pack. The other man was big, burly and mean-looking, but the cop had the authority... and the blackthorn staff. He crashed it down on his opponent's skull, dropping him cold.

Above us, meanwhile, the rotor-blades still whirled, their down-draught blasting us like a hurricane. But then, abruptly, the 'thrub' of the chopper's engines changed tone. I glanced up. It was slowly ascending. This was it. I leaped forward, knocking people out of my way, only for someone, suddenly, to snag me by my sleeve. I turned sharply. It was the cop. A grin touched his thin, grey lips.

"Fuck you!" I hissed, pushing him roughly away.

His expression transformed to stunned fury and with a wild roar, he lunged back at me, swiping with his truncheon. As blows go, they were puny and uncoordinated, and in retaliation, I pounded him mercilessly, slugging him head and body, my trusty right hook finally exploding against his jaw. To a man, the traders stood and watched, fascinated but also unnerved. They backed away en masse, when I rounded on them.

"Anybody else?" I asked.

None of them said anything.

I laughed scornfully. “Arseholes! You deserve this place!”

Then I turned and made my bid for freedom, grappling with the empty net as it soared upwards and moments later, being carried off into the night.

Don’t believe the James Bond films. Hanging onto something over a chasm which you know will certainly kill you if you drop into it, is unendurable agony. The wind had ice in it, and blew so hard that it made breathing difficult. My fingers were things of metal when finally we touched down – bloodless hooks, cramped and rope-burned. It was only twenty minutes later, but it felt like hours. I must have torn every muscle in my body during that agonising trip – hanging on as the air-streams buffeted me, as the screaming engines deafened me, as every part of me went slowly rigid with the terror of what awaited below. When we did land, on a rain-wet airfield far from anywhere I knew, I had to roll and tumble away to avoid detection. My legs would hardly hold me, they were shaking so badly, but I somehow made it, running for dear life and thrusting myself into the first wall of thickets I came to, ripping my flesh to shreds but jabbering prayers of thanks.

I needn’t go into too much detail about what the next few days involved. There’s a popular misconception that England is a small country with a gentle landscape, largely cultivated and noticeably lacking in wild and lonely places. Don’t believe it... or rather, do believe it and then try to make your way from one end to the other without any money, any map, only the clothes and training shoes you’ve been standing up in for the last week, and knowing that you can’t risk asking for help.

If you make it at all, I’d be impressed. I’m fitter than most, but even I found it arduous. I was being hunted for one thing... or so I assumed. Whether I was or not, it seemed it best to stick to the ditches and by-ways, sleeping at night in forest dens or the damp places under railway bridges. By the time I reached the north-west, I was starving, sodden, ragged and intolerably tired. I was also covered in nettle-stings and thorn-cuts. My feet were blistered, my skin raw and sunburned. Above all though, I was parched. I'd tried once to drink from a stream and had promptly been sick, chucking up what little sustenance there was left inside me. On another occasion, I went to a farmhouse and tried to beg a cup, but the woman living there set her dog on me, and it bit both my ankles before I could get away.

By the time I plodded into Manchester, I was little better than the thousands of tramps and deadbeats who already flood the northern capital's desolate streets. But at least that was cover of a sort. I was able to traverse the city unnoticed.

When I finally reached my own leafier neighbourhood, it was dark and raining, which matched my mood to a tee. Even then, my frustration grew worse when I stumbled up the garden path to the front door, and found the locks changed. A few moments later, I was by the front window, wiping away the trickling water. Through the smeared glass, I saw a family I didn't know in a room furnished in a manner I didn't recognise. A young mother, looking warm and pink in a dressing-gown and head-towel, was playing on the rug with two children in Donald and Mickey pyjamas. In an armchair behind them, a young father in slippers and tracksuit was sitting reading the Manchester Evening News.

I didn't try to force entry or even bang on the door and demand answers. I just walked away into the deluge. I'd ceased being able to pay my hefty mortgage several weeks previously and had been expecting repo at some stage. Not this quickly, admittedly, but then as far as the world was concerned, I no longer existed.

It took me an hour to make my way back into town, some uncertain idea steering me to the only other home I'd ever known... the gymnasium where I'd learned my trade. It was late-evening when I stumbled up the steps and entered, finding the old place dusty and ill-lit, but clearly still in use. The equipment was all there; the weights, the medicine balls, the swingbags, the sparring ring.

So was Barney... my old trainer, and a man who'd forgotten more about boxing than Don King would ever know. That had been years in the past, though, when a string of young toughs had risen to thoroughbred status under his guidance, when I'd been an up-and-coming banger with a glittering future. Barney was now fat and stunted, but above all old... so very, very old. From trainer-in-chief, he'd gradually been reduced to club dogsbody, to a guy they only allowed on the premises out of respect for his past. He was alone now, clearing up, his squat track-suited figure slowly working its way around the outside of the ring with a mop and bucket.

"Barn," I said from the doorway.

He glanced up, lifting his flat-cap to get a proper look at me. His wrinkled old face registered nothing, but then he was not an easy man to shock.

"How you doing, Kid?" he asked simply. He'd always called me 'Kid', almost as if he didn't know my real name. It was a boxing thing, I suppose.

I tried to smile. "Bit thirsty, Barn."

He laid the mop to one side. "Best come in then."

I limped towards him. He watched me carefully, as if sizing me up for my next opponent, no emotion visible.

"Things not so good?" he finally asked.

"'Fraid not."

"Better sit down." He took a stool from a corner of the ring. "Tea do? Just put the kettle on."

"Rather have water, if you don't mind."

He shrugged indifferently, and as I sat, lumbered away towards the kitchen door. My head dropped into my hands. A moment later, I heard the tap running... continuously. For longer than was necessary. Much longer in fact. It meant only one thing – Barney was on the phone to someone, using the splashing of the water to conceal it.

I felt too weak to react. Barney too? It was a shocking thought, but I was too numb to feel anything more than mild surprise. Why not Barney? He was part of society. More so now that he was old and useless and living on free food tickets. And wasn't it society they were trying to protect?

He came back in with a tall glass of water. I drank it in a single gulp, then wiped my mouth and glanced up at him. "So… how many people know about this, Barn?"

He gave it momentary thought, again without emotion. He wasn't remotely surprised that I'd sussed him. "More or less everyone," he finally said.

"Except me?"

He nodded slowly, almost sadly. "Yeah. Because lads like you never know, Kid."

I slammed my right fist into my left palm. I might have been drained, physically, emotionally, spiritually... but I knew I could uncage the beast one more time. It might be a beast born of synthetic chemicals, but it was a beast all the same. And what a beast.

"I'll tell you," I said to him, "they'll have to send an army."

He shook his head wearily. "They won't need to. There's already one here."

And as he spoke, that army trooped out to meet me... arriving in single file from the club changing-rooms. I watched it through disbelieving eyes, my spine slowly freezing. Of all the armies they could have sent against me, this was probably the only one I wasn't able to handle. Weak and undernourished though I was, if I'd been facing Baker's Wood's pretend police force and wasted inmates, I was just desperate enough to have beaten the hell out of the lot of them. But there wasn't much chance of that now. Not against this lot... the club's entire list of registered fighters.

They lined up in front of me as if ranked for inspection, all kitted out in shorts, vests, gloves and head-guards. Thirty of them at least, every weight represented, every standard, every race and colour. They only had one thing in common, a desire to take me down. And why not? I'd tarnished their game, their club, their creed. More important though, I'd once been an undefeated champ, a bench-mark all boxers hoped to surpass… a trophy to make their own.

The moment hope deserts you is a moment familiar to fighters; when you suddenly realise you've lost, when you've taken more damage than any man should, when all you've got left is your pride. Even the best of the best have experienced it. It sorts out the contenders from the also-rans, which is perhaps the reason I rose to my feet and returned their menacing glares eyeball to eyeball; it's perhaps the reason I chuckled scornfully, then turned, climbed up to the ring and vaulted over the ropes; why I shadow-boxed as I waited for them.

Barney wasn't hanging around. The last I saw of him, he was walking slowly towards the changing-rooms, dragging his mop behind him. Even if I'd wanted to call after him, I couldn't, because with only the clang of an invisible bell to warn me, my foes attacked.

Before I knew it, they were at the ropes. Two were coming over at the same time. I greeted them with rockets to their respective jaws, sending them flying backwards. They hadn't been ready for me... hell, they hadn't even got into the ring. But what the fuck, this was a real fight. They might as well learn that straight off.

I turned just in time to face my next opponent, who'd vaulted in behind me. It was Big Al, the token dull-witted heavyweight who'd been hanging around the gym for as long as anyone could remember. He was a southpaw and as broad and strong as an ox, but he was a real clubber. He launched a massive but ponderous left, which I dodged easily before hacking in a quick one below the belt, then slamming a right into his teeth. He went down like an oak tree felled.

Three down, twenty-seven to go. The odds were ridiculous and the tide soon turned. They now came over the ropes three at a time, the lighter guys dancing around me, jabbing here and there, the heaviers preferring to mix it toe to toe. I fended one bantam right across the ring, then put him on his back with a stinger to the chin. A young welterweight came next. He wove through my attack, and with fast hands planted me twice. Fast, yes; powerful, no. A crunching uppercut sent him sprawling into a corner.

But these were minor victories in the face of an increasingly savage bombardment. I turned and twisted, but gloves drove in at me from every side... and I was the one who wasn't padded, remember. Even when I did make a counter-punch tell, it injured me as much as them. Once again my knuckles were blasted to ruins, the old scabs long gone, new rents open to the bones. Even defence-work became an agonising chore.

I wouldn't have been up to such a task had I been in peak form, but in that weak, worn-out state, I soon became easy meat. Wallop after wallop made good contact. I blundered drunkenly among them, slipping and sliding in my own blood. My returns grew progressively weaker and less accurate. I hurt a couple more of them – busted a set of ribs here, smashed a nose there – but my head was now flying back and forth to their crisp blows, and before I knew it, my knees had gone.

The canvas hit me like an anvil. From some distant, sweat-filled place high above, I heard the referee:

"... eight, nine, ten..."

The roars of a population engulfed me...

As a professional warrior, 'last stand' culture always used to fascinate me – Davey Crocket at the Alamo, Custer at Little Big Horn – but now, having endured my own, I can assure you it isn't all they crack it up to be. To begin with, you don't go out in a blaze of glory, there's no restful oblivion afterwards, and no-one remembers you as a hero.

At least, I assume no-one remembers me, but then how would I know? I'm back in Baker's Wood – as you might have guessed – in the same room, looking out through cracked glass onto the same dirty, despondent streets. However, my situation has improved a little – a 'smidgin', you might say. Maybe I wasn't tough enough to go it alone in a world that hates me, but I'm still tougher than most of my colleagues in here.

Hence this.

It's a sort of life, I guess. But I wouldn't recommend it. All I can do is repeat my warning from before... don't make the mistake of being lured to Baker's Wood. I'm telling you, you won't get out again.

Certainly not on my shift.

Hitch

Gary Fry

She'd made her decision. The job interview was at 9:30 this morning, and if she was offered the position, at last she'd be free.

Mum was shouting from the hall passage: "Louise. *Louise*. There's the phone for you…"

She hadn't heard it ring; another heavy night of nebulous dreams she couldn't recall had given her one of her habitual headaches. Nevertheless, she wasn't long in flinging back the sheets, sitting up in her pyjamas and asking eagerly through the closed door, "Who is it?"

"Gavin."

Oh. Only Gavin. Climbing off the mattress, Louise said, "Tell him I'm busy getting ready. Say I'll ring him later, after I get back."

She heard her mum retreat with a disappointed stride across the bungalow, muttering, "You shouldn't mess such a nice lad about…" But Louise knew there would be no interference; she could be quite temperamental in response, quite the stereotypical teenager.

At least mum afforded her the privacy of her own room. Louise glanced around it now. TV/video combo; copies of some Stephen King novels her boyfriend had lent her, as well as the Hitchcock film, *Marnie,* he'd insisted she see.

God, what a name; imagine being saddled with that. She pulled it apart, played with its components. Hitch. She was hitched to life. Had there once been a hitch? If so, what had a cock to do with it?

She chuckled awkwardly, switching on her music centre. Her favourite band – *Stereophonics* – started playing, a number called 'I Wouldn't Believe Your Radio'. She sang along to the chorus as, in order to dress, she closed a gap in her curtains against the ugly countryside view. Having only one floor made her fearful that people might see.

Louise didn't really understand what Kelly Jones was on about, yet she loved his voice: naturally raw with an urbane sophistication. Louise was headed that way today: the vacancy at the chocolate manufacturer would take her into the city; she'd have money, control, maybe even transport if she could pass her test next year.

She thought then of her dad. The bugger. She'd told him about the opportunity, but he hadn't even contacted, let alone offered her a lift in the latest of his crappy cars.

Louise started stripping, sensing the guys on her posters watching, watching.

Kurt from *Nirvana* was okay; she could trust him. A shot of his torso cut off at the waist, his intense face with that dyed-blond hair and rugged glare sent a frisson up her naked spine. This was as alive as she felt these days. Sure, Gavin was likeable, yet his determination to go on to study A-levels and afterwards for a degree seemed like unnecessarily deferred gratification. She wanted excitement immediately! She was sixteen, after all: as good as an adult.

She examined herself in the hip-high mirror. Her breasts weren't as large as they could be, since she didn't eat a great deal, and certainly not sweets. However, she knew from the many gazes she drew that she was attractive. This felt like a power, though she wasn't sure whether it was a good thing; nor did she really understand how to use it or if she had the desire to. Despite so much attention, she often felt dead inside.

Buttoning a blouse over her snug bra, she shifted her scrutiny to a picture of the *Manics* in their grungy period, before guitarist Richey Edwards had vanished. She remembered being captivated by his behaviour during an interview: he'd carved words into one arm with a knife. Louise was too 'nice' (mum and friends had told her repeatedly) to do the same, but she understood the motivation. FOR REAL, she reflected, recalling the desperate rock star's message on his skin, and then supplemented her own phrase: LOOK AT ME.

She removed her pants to slip into a skirt. Now the only flesh visible in the glass was her face. Who did she resemble? She had her dad's large eyes. She narrowed her focus, at once appearing devious. If blokes were asking the questions at the headquarters in Leeds, she'd have an obvious advantage. She strapped on high heels which accentuated the shape of her carves and thighs.

Quite inexplicably, as she scrunched her hair before making her way through to the kitchen after stopping her CD, Louise experienced disquiet.

"He said good luck."

"Pardon? *Who* did?"

"Who do you think? Who just phoned?"

"Oh yes, sorry. I was miles away. I do have a lot on my mind, you know."

At the sink her mum scowled, holding a knife with which she was preparing food. Louise wasn't interested; typically she had no appetite, yet on this occasion she could ascribe it to nervousness, couldn't she?

"I do wish you'd rethink what you're doing, Lou'."

A wave of aggression snapped through her; she didn't care to be called Lou' – it made her feel like a child again, among other vague things. Nevertheless, she managed to control her attitude. Mum had seen enough violence for one life.

"I mean, what's wrong with staying on at school?"… boring, boring, boring… "Gavin's a nice lad. There aren't… there aren't many around, you know."

Yes, so dad was cruel to you, neglected me, and divorcing him was the best move you ever made, aside from this one, away from the city. But it's *dull*, mum. I'd also like to make up my own mind about dad. Okay, so he hasn't been in touch a great deal in the past decade, but he's still my dad, and I, I –

The words died in her mind, just as her spirit of rebellion had. She couldn't speak about anything complicated; she didn't have the language. Gavin had taught her many new phrases, yet although responding intuitively, she'd struggled to master them. She'd done well in her GCSEs, eight passes, three at grade A, but despite caring for ideas and the people they were often about, none of it fired her. She wanted to *live*, and the only way to manage that was to have money.

She gathered her handbag from the back of a battered chair they'd salvaged from the semi in Bradford; it was reassuringly heavy with her mobile and a purse full of coins rather than notes. Further education would mean staying at home, being skint; it would inevitably mean getting closer to her so-called boyfriend, whom she'd met in an English class and kind of drifted into a relationship with because that's what youngsters did, especially in such a 'nice' place where there was no one exciting…

She paced for the front door. "If dad phones…"

Immediately her mum turned on her, brandishing the knife. "What? Tell him to, to fuck off?"

The phrase shocked Louise; what was going through her mum's mind? She must be dismayed because, after years of struggling on social security with no paternal support, she imagined she was losing her only child. Fair enough. But still, when was the last time she'd heard her swear?

"I'm having to get the bus. I just thought he might have offered me a lift, that's all."

Her mum glanced away, continuing to chop the vegetables on the work surface, a carrot feeling the sting. Was it the onions that had brought tears to her eyes?

"Well, see you," Louise muttered, stepping outside.

She received no reply, not even a "good luck". Perhaps her mum knew something she didn't: that luck had nothing to do with life, that it was all choices made in difficult circumstances.

Louise suppressed this intuition; it disappeared deep in her brain along with other stuff that squirmed and disturbed her. She started walking for the one bus stop in the village.

***

As she followed the la ne, Louise reflected on her current life. She could appreciate the countryside, but only in an abstract way. It involved no emotion, no sensation. Further south, beyond a cluster of trees she didn't dwell upon, the tall buildings of Leeds scraped the sky, authoritatively erect, promising opulence and satisfaction, stimulation and control.

Her mind was confused at present; she was acting according to her feelings.

She understood her mum's point of view: the world was a dangerous place for women. Louise had read enough non-fiction on the subject of crime to realise that terrible things happened, things she'd rarely think about without experiencing discomfort. But more recently, feminism had transformed culture; Louise had enjoyed sociology classes dealing with these issues. So why not have a little of what men had enjoyed for so long: independence, power, control?

The word 'control' seemed to recur in her thought. She wondered why. Fields stretched out around her, soliciting her attention. Just then, a rabbit bounded across the uncut grass, a female presumably, chased by a buck whose habits and intentions were well-known. Oh well, that was nature: however dirty Louise regarded such behaviour, promiscuity was a way of preserving the species; the creatures couldn't help it. Perhaps this was why she was attracted to society: it offered organisation and structure. She hadn't always felt together during her turbulent teens.

Consulting her wristwatch, she'd reached a lane leading to the main road on which a bus was due in about five minutes. This was surely a final opportunity to change her mind. She had a choice, didn't she?

Behind her was a relatively secure everyday existence, but it was laden with a troubled past she was coming to realise she was eager to flee. Ahead was the future, and who knew what scary delights?

She hesitated for too long; the seconds ticked by –

A buffet of unruly wind decided her.

With tacit apologies to her mum, surely conquering dependence upon her, Louise struck off left towards the route that would deliver her to Leeds.

At this point, Gavin – with whom she'd never had sex, nor even offered a hand-job to – would have asked: To what extent are individuals free to choose their destinies? Is there such a thing as fate: that is, are we moved by higher forces? Or is life merely an accumulation of events, the way we handle them from day to day?

Was it any wonder she wished to get away?

But seriously, despite his academic aspirations, her boyfriend possessed a rural simplicity that didn't turn her on. He'd rather have a conversation than go dancing or race across a deserted moor in a reckless vehicle. At seventeen, he didn't even have a provisional licence, didn't seem interested; he probably believed that being mobile would contribute to global pollution or some such. Well, okay, that was fine – she herself wasn't irresponsible. She was just tired of the safety of it all.

The dry-stone walls and picket fences cut mercifully by. Her maternal grandparents had been country folk; she'd never met her dad's parents, though she knew they lived somewhere in Bradford, his father a bastard by all accounts, his mother timid and fearful. Louise didn't wish to end up like any of them. Yet maybe there was no escape. Perhaps Gavin was right. Basing his ideas on the psychology at which he'd excelled, he believed life to be something that happened which you couldn't control; it was as unpredictable in the town as it was elsewhere. But there were always choices: you had to consider often frightening options…

Oh God, no sooner had she quashed her mum's voice in her head than another stole in to take its place! She hurried on, sensing time slip past as well as a nearby wood whose thick gnarly trunks gathered secretive shadow.

It was then that she heard the groan.

Memory must be playing tricks on her. She'd associated the sound with the noise a human makes when… relieved or something. In fact it was mechanical, an engine approaching.

The bus.

Immediately she panicked. There was still about two-hundred yards to the end of the lane, and then a lengthy dash left to the shelter. She started running at once, her young body curiously thrilling to the chase. What was she thinking? It would be tragic if she didn't catch the only ride for an hour or so into the city; she'd miss her interview! However, her sense of arousal increased as she sprang along the tarmac. Her hearing must be affected; when she dodged around the corner onto the main road, the monstrous roar redoubled its effort: it was as if two vehicles were thundering by.

She flung out her arms, her bag clunking painfully against one hip. She was already considering the worst scenario – who she might call to rescue her: mum was no use, neither was her boyfriend – when the bulky single-decker charged beyond her, jetting back a shroud of toxic exhaust-fumes.

There were only a few passengers in the seats, their heads down as if they didn't care for the view. But Louise had managed to spot the driver: a man. Typical! He'd possibly seen her in her smart outfit, deduced where she was heading, and decided to compromise another female in the commercial marketplace. Indeed, he actually appeared to have accelerated as she'd emerged; he wouldn't be able to see her in his wing-mirror for all the smoke. The bastard.

Since nobody else from the miserable village was awaiting a lift, the bus surged on beyond the stop, grumbling like another human gesture: male arrogance.

"Stop!" she cried, far too late. "Hey, you… *you…*"

Anger suffused her to such a degree that she punched the air, imagining flaccid flesh within reach. But she mustn't grow irrational. If anything, this was her fault. She'd been dawdling, worrying about choice and other pointless matters. She shouldn't ascribe the disaster to men.

Now that was decided, she interpreted the departing whine of the engine as guilt: the audible atmosphere of a person's ignoble act. In fact she was exhausted from her exertions; her pulse flitted insanely in her wrists, or at least the right, her stronger side. She didn't know what she was thinking.

"Vehicles are phallic symbols," she heard either her mum or Gavin say in her throbbing skull. Both were capable of offering such an interpretation: mum had taken adult evening-classes in women's studies, while her boyfriend read Freud for fun. In any case, as Louise staggered to a halt beside the plastic bench and its single pole, she reflected on the nature of fate.

Perhaps she hadn't been meant to apply for the job, life conspiring to trap her in her former situation. Wrestling with the notions Gavin had tried to teach her, Louise realised that choice was a decision made between two options that presented themselves to you? It couldn't *generate* those conditions. Maybe the world was already carved up in favour of guys; perhaps chance, even in some chaotic universe where shit happened, was divined to limit feminine advancement.

Or of course, this could all be a load of bollocks.

The notion cheered her a little. Actually, these were intelligent enquiries: she might be a loss to academia, after all. A subjective reading of her current difficulties wasn't arbitrary; it was unavoidable – it involved the impact of events which demanded resolution. Somehow this *felt* right; her body stirred to the thought. As she wondered whether she could in fact reconcile herself to the past, she was jolted from her ruminations when a car honked its horn.

Louise jumped, as if she'd been prodded by something hard. In the wake of frustration, she'd slipped into a place of her own: somewhere within, writhing with questions, suspicion, and shapeless demons. She snapped out of it, twisting to glance at the cause of the noise.

Her dad was waiting at the kerb.

No, it might not be him, despite the fact that the hatchback was green, had tinted glass, and a raucous idle. In truth, she didn't know the difference between a Fiesta and an Astra, so this might not even be the same model as his, despite sharing its characteristics. She stooped at once to look through the near-side window. As she did so, the door arced open.

She felt so much taller than on previous occasions… Huh? What was *that* all about?

She heard a voice – low, gravelly, though a decade younger than she'd anticipated – say, "Get in!", and after a pause, "I saw what that bugger did. Wherever it is you want to go, I'll drive you. We could overtake the sod and give him what for."

'What for' – her mum used the term in quite a different context, often with embarrassment. However, at present, Louise couldn't contemplate. Another maternal phrase was filling her brain: *Never accept lifts from strangers!* But Louise was done with relying on others, wasn't she? She was sixteen, a grown-up; she was about to be considered for an important post, and the only way she could get there, short of phoning her unreliable dad, was to take up the man's offer. Even though she was carrying her mobile, she didn't have enough money for a taxi.

Oh, decisions! Procrastination had placed her in this position; she shouldn't exercise more of it. Should she?

The guy was extremely good-looking: like Kelly Jones from *Stereophonics*. Dark eyes, thick brows, tanned angular face, eleven o'clock shadow. Could someone so attractive harbour baser motives than giving her a ride? She didn't think so. Mindful of the time, Louise climbed inside the vehicle. Besides, something about the way he'd said "Get in!" had persuaded her to do so, as if she'd had no choice in the matter. He'd sounded authoritative, caring. She shut herself in and was whisked away.

***

"Hi," he said, changing gear – from third to fourth already.

"Hi," she replied, a tad nervous, though keen to uphold her unquestioned reputation for being 'nice', polite, grateful, a woman.

They barrelled along, surely above the speed limit. This was cool, exciting; at last she was with someone who was going somewhere. Yet Louise couldn't help feeling that she'd needed more preparation for this kind of activity, that being thrown into the situation precluded her need for control. Still, she had a deadline to meet, and even if at this rate, she'd be very early, it would be nice to annoy the bus driver. That must be what the man was intending. He surely wasn't this maniacal in ordinary circumstances.

"Where you heading?" he asked, his hand groping for hers – no, not that at all: the stiff knob of the gear-stick to enter cruise mode.

"Leeds," she told him, the monosyllable as much as her frantic breathing currently allowed: she didn't know whether she was aroused or afraid. Strapping on the seatbelt, she added, "The city centre. Th-thanks for this."

"No sweat."

That would make a change… But again, the thought was incongruous, bearing no relation to the present situation. She ought to ignore herself; she was feeling rather odd today – possibly residue of her waking headache. She said nothing.

Beyond a smooth curve whose oncoming blur included hedges and Lord knew what else, the single-decker had reared up. The man beside her accelerated harder, exhaling with joy or something more intense as the vehicles drew close.

"Wind down your window," he instructed, and Louise – incomprehensibly – was glad of the simple command. However, at once she did as she'd been bidden, the glass tumbling in a rigid sequence of jerks. A vicious breeze swept in, ruffling her hair like plump unsolicited digits. As the car overtook the bus, the man leaned her way, his left arm brushing her breasts that the belt was flattening further still; then he extended his index finger to jab through the vacant pane.

"Sit on that, fucker!" he yelled, and for the first time since she'd joined him, Louise had a moment to scrutinise her saviour in greater detail.

He was short, yet sturdy: shapely and muscular. He was dressed in jeans and a T-shirt, the casual wear of a guy on his day off; she wondered what he did for a living. Not much, if his vehicle was anything to judge by. But she shouldn't make assumptions; not everybody was as crooked and lazy as her dad. Louise thought the driver held his rude gesture rather longer than was necessary – the bus was receding in their wake, yet he kept his hand in front of her, that finger stuck up like something she didn't care to look at. She switched her scrutiny to the others: nothing on the third-left. He wasn't married; strangely, this didn't make her feel any more uncomfortable. He'd be all right; it was only a short journey.

At last he gripped the wheel securely, the deserted road opening out before them. Another stretch of trees gave way to a building – an isolated service station, selling confections and magazines. Louise was happy when the man spoke; it removed her attention from inscrutable matters.

"So, what's happening, eh?"

"What do you, you mean?"

"Er, why the big rush?"

She might ask him the same; despite having achieved his suggested aim, he hadn't slowed the car. Now their speed felt quite alarming, though she wouldn't say anything: he could easily take umbrage...

"I have a job interview," she explained, gripping her bag, feeling the corners of her mobile inside. When he didn't respond – had she offended him in some way? – she finished, "It's at nine-thirty. Do you think we can make it?"

His left hand again straying, the guy indicated the clock in the dashboard: it was 8:45. "Plenty of time," he said, a smile in his undeniably alluring voice, though she didn't glance to check. "Oh yeah, we've plenty of time."

For *what*? But she was being silly. In any case, he'd then asked a question.

"Do you live back there – in that village?"

Her feeling that she wanted her mum, or even Gavin, was quashed immediately. In fact, in her mind's eye, it was her dad's face she was seeing. She must answer promptly.

"Oh, I was, uh, just visiting. My parents, they're divorced, see. They live apart."

"I get it." He didn't seem surprised; perhaps he'd emerged from similar circumstances. "What's the job, then?"

She'd already lied – might she do so again, and if so, why? At any rate, she felt more comfortable saying, "It's just a Sunday post. In the market. I'm, I'm still at school."

"Oh, really," he replied, and it was surely only a quirk of her brain that had her attaching excitement to his tone. Why had she told him this – to increase the difference between them, the better to evade any scary flirtation? Or did she in fact crave his attention? He was very attractive, an older man. Despite her nebulous concern, she discovered that she was quite aroused. Then he added, "What are you studying?"

"Psychology, principally." It was her boyfriend's stilted phrase that had supplied the detail, yet all the while she was thinking: I don't want *him*; he's too nice. Give me life and loving – I'd no longer need to be a world-beater. The job wouldn't matter.

If only the driver didn't own such rubbish transport.

"Repression and all that?" he surprised Louise by announcing; maybe he was smarter or more sensitive and vulnerable than she'd guessed. "Tell me about it…"

Was he issuing an instruction, or expressing regret, presumably about his own life? The comment seemed too ambiguous, like her presence here just now. Did she want him to chat her up or not? Was she teasing him or being deliberately evasive? She was either flattered or fearful, yet couldn't mark which.

In order to transcend all this troubling speculation, she asked, "What do *you* do? For a living, I mean."

His stomach grumbled, an animal noise that had her looking down too far: at his groin. He caught her glance. Smiled.

"Need something to satisfy it," he said as she snapped her head forward – too quickly; he'd surely read something into the reaction. She must appear nervous, but she was able to placate her concern by thinking he'd meant his stomach.

"I'm a…property developer and, er, landlord," he went on, stiffening his posture a little. "Don't be fooled by this old wreck.

It's just a c-courtesy vehicle while my, my Porsche is at the garage being repaired."

She'd heard such lies before, from her dad especially: that capacity to act on the hoof she'd learned was a particular skill of humans, or men exclusively, as her mum would argue. Gavin never lied; he was honest, yet in his case it was a virtue born of simplicity, niceness. This had never done anything for Louise.

She'd play the driver along; after all, she hadn't been honest with him either, had she? The car was certainly old, though she'd seen worse on the road. In fact he might not be lying. She could hedge her bets.

"Really?" she said, sounding impressed. "Do you have lots of…" – money – "…houses?"

"Enough. In fact I need to stop off at one on our way, if that's okay. Got to pick something up."

They'd reached a roundabout. Ahead was Leeds, to the left and right squalid suburbs. He was already indicating; her heart rate stepped up. She didn't reply, yet couldn't control her jagged breath.

"Don't worry," he explained, steering towards shadows and buildings interspersed by green patches of land. "I'll be quick."

Don't worry. I'll be quick. All she needed to hear now was, *Be a good girl*. But her thought was veering into wild territory. She ought to distract herself, sing a song in her mind. She trawled for a catchy tune, something by *Oasis* or *Blur*. Tumbledown dwellings flanked the street, yet here at a junction was an incongruous sign: TWAIN FOREST, it read; 1 MILE.

At once a melody came to her involuntarily, but it wasn't one she'd have chosen: *If you go down to the woods today, you're sure of a big surprise…* She was dispirited to realise how like a child she suddenly felt – frightened, helpless, and manipulable. She shouldn't worry. It was broad daylight. The guy had turned off in advance of parking up outside any of the grotty semis they were currently passing; he would skip out to collect rent or some such, before returning to complete his kindly offered lift. There was no reason to panic. He couldn't lock her in. He must be what he'd claimed; if that was true, it might be profitable to develop her conversation with him.

Negotiating the council estate, he eventually pulled the car into the kerb of a cul-de-sac whose bulbous head was tarmac-ed and bore only a single escape route: the dark throat of an alley overhung by prickly foliage. The housing was pretty depressing, its background a greying sky threatening rain. Wind clanged against the windows, bringing the humming heater to her attention; at least it was warm in here, her fingers tingling. There were no people about. The guy wouldn't do anything obscene! But then he unlatched his door, the clunk dragging her reflection back from the past… She saw now that he hadn't been wearing his seatbelt, more evidence of his recklessness. His hips stirred on the greasy seat. Louise couldn't move, didn't wish to, yet she knew she was about to receive instruction; this had happened before.

"Don't go anywhere," came the somewhat unexpected advice. He'd snatched the keys from the ignition, murdering the heat. "I won't be long."

And he clambered out.

He *couldn't* be long; he was around five-foot-seven. Everything was always in proportion, as some of her schoolmates claimed, though Louise had never sought evidence for this. Or had she? Images bombarded her; she opened her eyes wider to watch the man walk on, up the weed-choked path of number 24, to halt at an entrance flaking paint and splinters of wood. *He was dead fit!* – that was another of her pals' favourite phrases. His denims clung to his legs as tightly as the gloves her mum wore to wash up.

With his rear to her, Louise couldn't see any bulges. However, once he re-emerged – he was presently prising a key into the lock with covert exactitude; it popped back out; he inserted it anew – she could examine his crotch. Well, it's what young women did these days, she reckoned, despite her mum's inexplicable cry of horror in her skull. Louise would learn how sexy, or possibly how sexual, the man was. The prospect held her in the chair for several seconds.

***

He'd been gone nearly a minute – it was now 8:56 – before her rational sense returned. Would she be on time for her interview? The question seemed loaded in the guy's favour: without him, how would she make the remaining mile or so into Leeds? Asking her dad was a possibility, but she didn't imagine he'd be up yet, let alone willing to venture out on request. Anyway, how would she call him and not attract unwanted attention should her rescuer return? She wasn't entirely sure of where she was either, and could hardly give directions even if he did answer the phone. He was *so* lazy; he didn't work officially, just sold junk on the black market, possibly even soft drugs. Of course her boyfriend wouldn't entertain the proposal of smoking dope, however much she'd been tempted to try it. He reckoned the attendant world to be peopled by seedy men, liars, the unscrupulous, and the violent.

Was Gavin right?

Dad was certainly quick with his fists, and rarely for any noble reason.

Was the driver of the car (whose name she suddenly realised she hadn't asked; still, she hadn't provided him with her own) of a similar stripe?

No, he couldn't be; he'd brought her to one of his houses. Nevertheless, she wondered. Her mum had rented from private landlords for years; they wouldn't have been able to afford to live in the bungalow and the village otherwise. In any case, Louise was sure none of these guys would ever simply let themselves into a property: tenants had rights, after all.

She stirred on the seat.

Alternatively, if he was up to no good, would he have left her alone in this vehicle? She might flee at any moment. However, knowing he had a Porsche precluded a hasty, irrational decision. He clearly fancied her; that almost subliminal look they'd exchanged when his stomach had rumbled had been charged with attraction – she *knew* it. It was odd how much could be conveyed without words. And when he *had* spoken, weren't his comments ambiguous enough to be open to other interpretations?

It was such intuition that unsettled her. In fact language, collapsed into sense impressions, was informing her interpretation of the present. She'd read frequently about serial killers, how they drove around trawling for a potential victim. *Anybody* wouldn't do; the person in question had to meet a specific criterion. Perhaps the driver possessed a fetish for schoolgirls...

The thought alerted Louise, and more so because to some extent she'd been an accomplice in fostering this notion. What subtle processes had been going on between her and the man? Ironically, if she'd studied further education, maybe she'd understand, might be currently running away, to hell with the job, free...

Hey, hold on, *hold* on. It was her dad's voice in her head, reassuring her. Why should this be? Whatever the reason, she was grateful. She remained in the car, staring at the semi. She glanced again at the dashboard clock: it was 8:58.

What could the guy be doing? What was he collecting? Was he a ruffian, demanding money with menaces? Louise had witnessed that sort in films. He might have been carrying a weapon... But of course she knew he wasn't: those tight pants would have surely revealed any hidden tool. She needed to check him out when he came back, and not only for potential romantic purposes.

A suspicion emerged from a fractious part of her brain.

Might he be seeking an item inside?

She jerked so rigorously, her knee clanged the glove compartment, forcing it open on damaged hinges. It clattered loudly, causing her to glance around the cul-de-sac, checking for onlookers. But it remained deserted; only the shadowy alley promised intrusion. The residents of the neighbourhood must be still in bed, all as bone-idle as her dad. Or...or highly sexed.

At once Louise looked down at the objects which had spilled onto the dropped lid. Actually they were somewhat innocuous: a few dusty tapes of out-of-date bands, a number of legal documents, and a nearly full packet of Polos, the mint with a hole. The wrapping at the head of the tube was splayed like liquid, opening on to a thin white vacant column. She reached for the sweets, yet faltered, loath to touch them. The fact that these were invariably what perverts used to persuade youngsters into their transport was, bizarrely, less terrifying than another realisation which shocked her like the touch of moist flesh, like the breakdown of a established relationship on account of some ignoble act, like a warped violation of her body.

She snatched open the door and jumped out.

"Be a good girl," she heard amid the clatter of her footfalls as she raced for the gap at the head of the tarmac. She twisted her torso; his vision smeared, while she heard other voices: *Don't worry. I'll be quick.* Each of the comments must be imaginary, since there was nobody in pursuit. She plunged between spiky tendrils of cruel nature, her handbag swaying like the beat of time, drawing her back, filling her mind with horrifying implications.

Her dad had driven her into a wood. He'd –

"No!" That was certainly her own exclamation; she tried to fill the gaping void inside her with a sensible rationale.

The hatchback (just like her dad's: the same colour, the same tinted glass, the same insidious idle when it was running) couldn't be a supply vehicle from any garage because it bore personal artefacts, grubby with neglect. Louise was sure she'd seen a driver's licence within the stack of papers: had the name beneath the plastic sheath (...which *he'd* never used, the dirty fucker...) been Richard Porter? Why had he transferred all his music to a car he'd use for only a few days? How had the cassette boxes become dirty so soon?

Of course the answer was obvious: it was *his* vehicle. *That* was his house. He hadn't merely happened to be driving through her village – he'd been looking for someone suitable, and having unexpectedly chanced upon an ideal type, he was now searching for something to force upon her...

He'd lied. Her dad had lied. They were *all* liars, as her mum had insisted, yet Louise would beg to differ about Gavin. Oh, she wished her boyfriend was with her now. He was no fighter, but his presence would certainly be sufficient: he was good, nice, a worthy man.

Louise hardly knew what she was thinking.

The end of the claustrophobic alley gave on to a sports field bounded by closely gathered trees. However, as she slowed to catch her frantic breath, she could hear noises beyond the deserted expanse of grass: muted transport passing, roaring filthily. This was coming from the left. It was ludicrous, though necessary, to consider that she might still make her interview. If she reached the road, she could perhaps hail a taxi, or maybe more buses were in operation in this region of Leeds.

But the city now frightened her.

A bird chirruped in the proximate wood; heading through there was the quickest route to so-called civilised culture. Between trunks which creaked in a rampant breeze, a petrol station was visible. Behind her stood the council estate; moisture hung in the cool air. She required shelter, ought to move on. If someone was following, she wouldn't check, just keep jogging, her mobile banging against one leg. The football field (a game her dad hated, preferring less competitive recreations such as pubs and bookies and... and...) fell away beneath her severe strides. She entered the darkness of the natural world, feeling unexpectedly safe.

It was a choice she'd made: to flee. A choice embedded in the context of her life. She was hitched to circumstances; there *had* been a hitch –

She wouldn't pursue the thought any further.

But did she have this option?

She stepped across broken autumn branches, leaves browned with the brittleness of age. She was travelling back – *No*, she'd travelled forwards, after hitching with the driver of the green car, its glass smoky to prevent too much public interference...

Louise believed she heard an engine nearby, but when she glanced around, shaking inexorably, there was nothing: only the nearly invisible shuffle of creatures at play on the earth, performing what their biology decreed. It wasn't so bad in this place, after all, despite the imposition of ideas she didn't wish to address. Yet the location seemed to press these to her attention, even though she wished to keep her distance from them: here in a clearing were tyre-tracks. Did someone older use this plot as his preferred venue, conveying his twisted society to another young unwitting victim? He would get his cock out as the car idled, ready to be driven on lest anyone intervene…

"Don't worry. I'll be quick." And then, "Be a good girl."

Louise halted, squatting on a bed of soil. She was crying, large tears falling like the rain that began to plop through the canopy of vegetation, setting the ground alive with threat. But there was no one behind her. She'd left Richard Porter to his bewildered return. He might grow angry, might adjust whatever item he'd retrieved from the house, and get in his vehicle to hunt. Curiously, Louise sensed a tiny thrill in response to this possibility, one she suppressed immediately, yet which prompted her to wipe her eyes, part the mouth of her bag, fish out her mobile in order to check for an adequate reception. There was no clear line – fucking culture! – yet once she'd stood and drifted closer to the petrol station on the road beyond the fringe of trees, the connection crackled: she could make a call.

The LCD display read 9:03; there was still time to reach the chocolate manufacturer. Nevertheless, as Louise dialled, she understood at once that her priorities had altered. She waited within the lip of the wood, watching a motorist zoom past her, honking his horn with impatience. The social world stank! She knew it now; it was what her mum had tried to tell her repeatedly, and also what Gavin had hinted at in his usual tactful way.

The phone commenced pulsing, matching the determined rhythm of her own physiological prompt to action. Her mum's and her boyfriend's wisdom could no longer be denied. Previous experience shouldn't be ignored; it needed confronting, interpreting – it was a choice one made: to ignore and suffer, or the honest, emancipating alternative, however painful it would be… But Louise knew she had sufficient strength.

As the summoning was broken and someone answered, she drew breath to speak.

"*Hello*?" A man's tone, gruff and inconsiderate.

"Hello… dad," she said, sensing his breath in her ear, almost tangible.

"Lou' – Louise?" He'd betrayed himself already, using the name he'd deployed when she was a child. Or could he be groggy, having just awoken?

"Are you still in *bed*?"

She'd asked the question emphatically, suppressing anger. She wasn't in fact convinced by her vague recollections, yet there was a way of discovering for certain. It would involve meeting him; simultaneously, she could test his devotion, his commitment, or at least the degree of his guilt.

"No, no, I've b-been up a while," he explained, the repetition and stammer persuading her that he was lying. Why did he have to pretend to be a decent man? He clearly wasn't – he'd neglected her, had been cruel to mum in Louise's presence. It was as if he thought he could always convince her with language, the way he was trying now. The way he'd tried in the past. His seedy, duplicitous brain growing audibly aroused, he added, "What's up? Where are you?"

So in a calm, measured voice, she told him. She mentioned the job again, ignored his irresponsible sighs, instructed him to drive swiftly to the – yes, she could read the sign across the road: TWAIN SERVICES.

She'd made her decision. Now, ending the call with a firm forefinger, all she had to do was to wait.

***

It had happened, if it had happened at all, in a wood similar to this one. She'd been six or seven years old; she *must* have been – that was just before mum had left him, taking Louise to live in difficult conditions.

Now she'd acknowledged the fact, images bombarded her, like a dream sequence in any of the films Gavin enjoyed, directed by his favourite artists. Hadn't he described one of King's novels similarly – *Gerald's Game*, was it called? She hadn't read the book yet, dismissing it immediately as trash, but were there more insidious reasons for her avoidance?

At any rate, she'd managed to bind her random recollections together into something that resembled a narrative; the implications were terrifying, yet she entertained them all the same.

He'd picked her up from school irregularly. "Get in!" he'd instructed, not authoritatively, rather urgently, as if he had pressing matters to attend to. He'd often carried sweets, a little treat in advance of driving to the wood where he'd talk to her with a furtive tone before, sweating profusely, asking her to do *that* with his –

Louise threw out her right arm, as if she wished to disown it. The action assumed a horrible pumping action, a movement mimicked by the swaying of the trees around her. But she couldn't hold nature responsible; back then, it was the place to which she'd fled in her mind, a rarefied, clean region that didn't involve people. Even now, she saw a man in the forecourt of the petrol station jamming a nozzle in the tank of his car – at least her dad hadn't gone this far…

She was extremely confused; her brain was loaded with symbols and skewed memory. None of it might actually have occurred, it could all be a projection derived from a modern culture obsessed by the issue of child abuse. Nevertheless, this reading *felt* right. The deadness in her body had been alleviated to some extent; she was mobilised to retaliation. She had a choice to make.

Should she continue to hide in the shadow of the wood, or re-emerge in a society whose complex vicissitudes had conspired to render her empty, hungry, dismissive of goodness? All she knew was that she no longer wanted what she'd desired less than an hour ago; the driver who'd picked her up had done her a favour, regardless of his ultimate intentions. She should pace out into the road, cross for *Twain Services*. She'd be exposed of course, and if Richard Porter was on the prowl, he was sure to see her. Yet so what? Her dad would arrive soon; somehow she'd tackle them both simultaneously.

She'd made her decision. Louise felt assertive as she slid through a stile onto the kerbside, awaiting a gap in the traffic. A guy passing in a dark saloon looked at her long and hard, obviously attracted, but she didn't want this attention now; indeed, it was like an intrusion. She hurried over the tarmac, her high heels stabbing like knives. When she'd made the opposite side, she hesitated, consulting her wristwatch: it was 9:10.

Her dad lived nearby, in a terrace house in a scummy area of Leeds; he couldn't be much longer getting here. However, she rushed to the entrance of the store, checking behind her repeatedly as more vehicles raced up and down the road. The council estate on which Richard Porter certainly lived was to the left; if he was eager to recapture her, he'd emerge from the same direction.

Louise didn't enter the building immediately: she was keen to be spotted. It was broad daylight – several other motorists had parked to fill up. What could happen in public? Men like that, and she tentatively included her dad, needed seclusion to do their worst. She waited, watching. A minute slashed by. Then a green hatchback pulled into the concrete forecourt, halting against a far wall.

Her heart rate stepped up at once, more proof if she required it that her body knew what her consciousness had repressed. Yes, this was what it was like: hadn't Gavin said something to that effect? Hadn't her mum? Fragments of education by proxy teemed through Louise; her choices had been made by necessity, cruel facts she couldn't evade. Life had happened to her – she *must* deal with the consequences. Nevertheless, since the tinted glass of the idling car revealed no clue as to its occupant, she trembled anew. She was staring directly at the shadowy occupant who, for several seconds, didn't move; she sensed a shiver creep up her chilled spine. The social world bred monsters, she suddenly understood. She wanted as little as possible to do with it in future. But first she needed to handle its insidious residue. The driver was climbing out of his seat.

It was Richard Porter. The Astra or Fiesta had fallen silent. He was gazing straight back her way.

Was this fate, forces beyond her reckoning delivering him? Sure, choices were indeed made in life, yet these involved circumstances outside of your control, possibly divined... Louise sensed the heavens churn, though the rain had dried up almost as suddenly as it had dropped. Was this a sign of something?

But she shouldn't let such speculation get in the way of handling the situation.

Despite her rage, she shunted open the shop door and struggled inside. Perhaps her retreat was due to doubt; she didn't know that her ostensible saviour was actually guilty of anything, did she? In fact she was more certain about her dad, who'd surely arrive soon. She turned away to address a rack of magazines, the first a women's regular whose cover read I SURVIVED SEXUAL ABUSE! She glanced elsewhere, at a tray displaying rows of sweets, then at a section of shelves bearing kitchen utensils: can-openers, corkscrews, cheap-looking innocuous cutlery...

She dodged along one aisle as someone followed her in; the man hadn't left his vehicle near a pump, so he might browse without arousing the suspicion of the girl at the till. The store was U-shaped: in order to get out, you had to circle innumerable shallow products, the kind Louise had always wished to own, though for which she'd lacked funds. This delusion crumbled as she headed towards the till attendant... who could only be her own age; did she work here alone at night, with so many potential creeps about? Louise's sight grew distorted; she stumbled for the exit. A face behind her appeared bewildered, frowned and maybe smiled. She wouldn't linger to discover. She burst outside, her coin-heavy bag almost toppling her with inertia. Yet she maintained her balance.

Another green hatchback had manoeuvred to halt beside the first.

Her *dad.* The criminal or her saviour; she might make the same claim of the guy chasing her. She grew perplexed, hurtled into the centre of the concrete. As footsteps strayed beyond her, the second car released a tall, brutal figure, scars across each cheek from one drunken brawl or another. Or could these have been caused by lengthy fingernails? Had he ever stopped? Is that why her mum had left him – had she *known*?

The thought frightened Louise, though at the same time she could appreciate the efforts that had been made to protect her. She swivelled on the spot, seeing the man who'd picked her up this morning strolling for his vehicle. He was glaring her way, as her dad was. Then they'd formed a perverse stationary triangle, ten yards between each of them.

Bizarrely, viewing the quiet wood in the peripheries of her vision, she wished her boyfriend was with her; despite his limited activity, he'd have known how to handle the problem. Yet his former support might be enough. He was nice, strong, noble; he clearly understood a thing or two about the darker side of human nature.

"Lou-Louise?" said her dad, his stammer born of confusion: he was glancing at the other guy, violence ripe in his expression.

Good. That was perfect. She said, "You made it. Quickly. You, you always did, didn't you?"

His face grew puzzled, but that look of aggression refused to dissipate. She might press home her psychology.

Directly on cue, as if nature was working in her favour, Richard Porter said, "Hey, what's going on? *Who's* this? Why'd you run, eh? I was only trying to help!"

Sure, and what's that lump in your pocket? She could have been asking this of her dad in the past, yet the guy did have something in those tight jeans, something that hadn't been there earlier: whatever he'd fetched from his house.

Louise ignored him, switched her attention to the other beast. She recalled the weird moment of unarticulated body language she'd experienced only a quarter-of-an-hour earlier, and realised how to elicit a confession from him. It would mean risking the safety of the possibly guiltless guy to her right, but so be it: she'd given up being considerate, being nice. That was how her dad had once guaranteed her silence, wasn't it? Be a good girl, a good girl, a good girl…

She couldn't hold in her fury any longer; still, she must perform the process carefully, the better to learn the truth.

"D-Dad, this chap picked me up this morning. I missed my bus, and conveniently, he happened to be in the right place at the right time. He said he'd give me a lift to my job interview, and without thinking of the, the danger, I got in his car."

She paused, examining the pair of them. Knowing what was coming, her dad, if he was in fact decent, didn't appear as angry as he should; conversely, Richard Porter was bouncing beside his wing-mirror, that long flat round item in his pocket jerking to and fro. They both clearly anticipated the accusation she was about to make, were similarly silent. As she prepared to speak, she could barely suppress a painful smile of victory.

"Halfway into the city centre," she announced, switching her sight from one to the other, "he tried to molest me."

"No!" The accused driver was horrified, either actually innocent or shocked at having his intentions revealed so coldly.

Her dad, however, was trapped between two habitual emotions. If, as Gavin had told her, the body was the site in which all facts were located, then what had been done to her – what she'd *felt* was the case – was clearly visible. He appeared both furious and ashamed. His hands clenched into fists, his gaze dropped. A moment later, his eyes returned to hers, and as she heard a car door being wrestled open, she flicked her glance right, indicating the coward, suggesting that much could be corrected if her dad did the right thing now.

"I'm having none of this shit, thank you," Richard Porter snarled, climbing behind the steering wheel, his fingers groping at his waist. He might be suddenly conscious of what he was carrying; alternatively, he could be genuinely aggrieved. At any rate, Louise was about to find out. In response to her knowing ministrations, her dad was thumping across to the vehicle that was like his own, set to do what he did best: hit somebody, as opposed to hitting on somebody; put his evil to some use.

He caught the guy before he'd shut himself within, dragging him out by his cropped hair, unmindful of the way his limbs contorted as he was flung to the ground. Her dad commenced kicking Richard Porter, first in the crotch, then the head, now the arms and legs. Blood splayed and splattered. Incomprehensible sounds of pain were forced from his lips: "Ow! Ugh! Argh!" The thing in the man's pocket never shifted.

A small crowd had gathered to each side of Louise – other drivers, the girl from the till point – though she didn't acknowledge any of them. Disturbingly, she was fused with her dad's activities, relishing every connection, enjoying the crunch of flesh and bone… But this was *wrong*; it was her mum's voice in her mind, and *she* should know: she'd suffered enough of this very behaviour.

"Okay, stop it!" Louise yelled over the buzz of shock around her, above the sounds of her dad's repeated assaults.

He'd stooped to start punching. He was saying, "Do that to a young girl, would you? How *could* you? It's not, not *right*!"

Louise realised this was the typical attitude of a perpetrator when confronted by his failings in another: denial, projection, rage. She would have to stop him; he was going to kill the guy who might not even be the same.

She paced to the dispute, gripped her dad before he could rain any more blows on the vulnerable skull. His movement squirmed from her in such a slippery way that initially she was loath to touch him again. It had reminded her of… But she blocked the impression; a savage gust of wind renewed her attempt. Eventually, screaming "Dad!" in a manner she'd never exercised previously – since she'd always been too nice, too scared – he relented. Looked at her. Then away. Stood and retreated a bemused distance.

The gathering of onlookers, many of them men who hadn't intervened, let out an audible gasp of horror.

There was red everywhere. Louise kneeled to assess the extent of the damage, feeling dismayingly responsible. She sensed her dad staring on, like a child who was unable to control his passions. He seemed frozen in the act – what had he *done*? And the worst part for him obviously was the fact that he had *two* victims before him on the floor: one bearing external wounds, the other with scars inside.

Excellent. She wanted him to suffer, to understand to some degree what it felt like to receive. She wasn't interested in excuses, tales of his difficult childhood with unloving, disciplinarian parents, or any of the other crap such individuals generally produced. Life was something that happened which you couldn't control; there were always choices…

Steadily, so as not to exacerbate Richard Porter's injuries, she reached for his groin. She hoped her dad was watching, hoped he realised what it meant for her to commit this act; she was sobbing, her handbag dangling in the cuts and developing bruises of the smashed, liquid torso. A siren struck up; someone had called the law, either from a mobile or the store telephone. It didn't matter: Louise was determined to exact her own form of justice. She hadn't been deceived; her body knew it.

She pushed one hand into the tight denim pocket to discover what the instrument was.

It was cold and metal, larger than her palm.

She removed it.

A weighty penknife.

It possessed a folded blade, lethal enough to achieve whatever horrendous acts Richard Porter had been planning. That made him worse than her dad, didn't it? But Louise wasn't convinced by such culturally-decreed relativity. All crimes against females were wrong, whether or not they involved a physical attack. What had the guy intended? Rape under threat? The *fucker*. Yet her dad was, in her mind, equally culpable.

She stood and turned to him. He appeared sheepish, wiping the blood from his clothing as a police panda stole shrieking onto the forecourt, letting out two uniformed officers: a man and, mercifully, a woman. The siren was cut, killed.

Stepping closer so as to make the moment as intimate as he had once required her to be and to keep the blade from the sight of the police, Louise made a threatening gesture with the penknife. She'd learned how to convey information without the necessity of words, from one body to another, abused to abuser.

She glanced at her dad's groin. She waved the blade from side to side. Then she looked back into his face.

He knew. He knew *she* knew. He nodded and gazed elsewhere. With his record, he'd probably be in trouble with the authorities, yet this could have been far more severe. But she wouldn't press for that. Punishment was about correction; her mum and Gavin, both humanists, had argued thus. Louise believed she'd achieved exactly what she'd intended.

It had been a choice made in difficult circumstances, yet a choice all the same, and – she trusted – a very wise one.

***

Decisions, decisions…

Louise was alone at home, sitting beside the telephone in the kitchen while the vegetable lasagne – her mum's speciality – cooked with alluring smells. She'd already called the company, apologising for missing the interview and explaining that she wouldn't be pursuing her application. Now she had a bunch of A-level forms beside her on the table. The course was due to start at the local school the following week, and all she was required to do was contact one of her former teachers to guarantee a place in each of the classes she'd like to study: psychology, sociology, and English.

Yet should she choose this?

Gavin was coming around soon; Louise had invited him for a meal. After several hours at the police station giving evidence, she was very hungry, yet only for food – her thoughts about grand individual achievement had vanished along with her flagrant self-regard. She'd changed into a sweater and baggy trousers, tossing into the clothes-basket her short skirt and blouse, which would of course be washed, ironed, returned to her bedroom drawers as if by magic.

She stood, accessed the sink; a knife lay amid innumerable pans. She reached for it, feeling her body thrill to a power that scared her, yet was under control.

She hadn't yet told her mum about the events of the day; it was Louise's turn to protect her, and with her boyfriend's help as any legal proceedings developed – she'd tell him first about her day – she might achieve this.

It was a crazy world, the countryside thrumming audibly around her. When a car pulled up outside the house – just the taxi from the peaceful village bringing the two reliable, loved people in her life: she from essential shopping, he from reading some difficult text or other – Louise replaced the utensil and, whistling a favourite tune, strayed for the handset. It would be nice to be making the request as they entered.

Without further hesitation, her circumstances forcing her to act, she chose to dial.

The Memory of Joy

Eric Brown

There is no pain so great as the memory of joy in present grief
Aeschylus

The last glimpse I had of my daughter was when I left the house and crossed to the car. Ella was dancing around on the lawn, playing with her dog. She was wearing knee-length dungarees and a red tee-shirt, and her spontaneous, five year-old laughter filled the air with joy.

She looked up and smiled at me.

I treasure that last smile.

I climbed in behind the wheel and sat for a while, going over what I had to get from the artist's supply shop in Oxford. I should have set off immediately. The future would have been very different, then.

But I hesitated, ordering my errant memory.

I turned the key, started the engine.

In the brief minute I delayed before setting off, Ella must have moved from the lawn.

I never saw her.

I backed the car down the gravelled driveway.

I felt the slight resistance, conducted through the bodywork of the car; then I felt the gentle crunch, a faint popping detonation, and it came to me that I had run over one of Ella's plastic toys, her tricycle or doll.

I swore and opened the car door.

In retrospect I realise that that action was the last my old self would make – the old self of blithe contentment, of innocence. Nothing would be the same again.

I glanced back along the length of the car. At the very second I beheld my daughter's outstretched legs – without really comprehending the evidence of my eyes – I heard my wife scream.

Laura was standing at the front door. She had watched Ella run from the lawn, dart behind the car. Our daughter had knelt, then got down on her belly to examine something that caught her childish interest, a ladybird, perhaps.

Laura had seen all this through the lounge window. She had stood transfixed, paralysed, knowing what was about to happen – granted, as it were, a foresight of the tragic inevitability of events played out before her – and had been unable to do a thing about it.

Laura's scream brought home the truth that my eyes had refused to acknowledge.

Framed in the doorway, between the beauty of hanging baskets, abundant crimson phlox and trailing fuchsia, she raised her hands to her face and wailed.

Munch. *The Scream.* Pure Horror.

I moved from the car. I caught my wife. We dropped to our knees, holding each other. We crawled across the gravel, towards the car, towards Ella, and we lay on the ground, still clinging to each other, and without looking upon the remains of our daughter we reached out as one and grasped her sun-tanned, dungaree'd leg.

That was how the neighbour found us later – I have no idea how much later – and called for an ambulance.

***

Laura spent the next three days in the local hospital, out of it on a powerful cocktail of tranquillisers. I refused the balm of barbiturates. Conscious, the horror was bad enough. I did not want to leave myself prey to whatever demons might haunt me in the twilight world of delirious semi-consciousness.

I spent the next few nights with a friend in the village. My brother came down from Yorkshire, the lineaments of his face pulled into unfamiliar lines of grief, and I experienced a gnawing guilt for all the pain I'd caused.

I found myself giving thanks, then, that my mother had passed away the year before. Ella's death would have destroyed her.

Laura's parents had died years ago, before we married. They

too were spared the pain, and I the guilt of burdening them with pain.

I visited Laura every day, spending hours beside her bed. For the first two days she was unconscious. On the third, I arrived to find her sitting up, staring at the opposite wall.

Staring...

My transit across her line of sight brought not a flicker of response. I sat on the bed and gripped her hand. Nothing. She looked ten years older, drained, grey, her eyes haunted and empty.

I found myself unable to speak. Words were beyond me – crude, rude things wholly inadequate to the task of communicating my complex thoughts and feelings.

At last I mouthed platitudes. How much I loved her. How much I was sorry.

I told her that Dan, my brother, had suggested we sell the house. I told her that I was putting it on the market and looking around for something else.

Nothing, not a flicker of response. I was concerned for Laura, of course – but I would be lying if I denied that I was concerned also as to her reaction. Would her pain and recriminations target me?

Later, sitting in the darkness of my studio at the bottom of the garden, it came to me that, loath though I was to be the butt of my wife's accusations, a part of me would welcome the blame, for only when we shoulder the burden of responsibility can we be granted absolution.

***

On the third day in hospital, Laura attempted to take her life.

She climbed from bed, swung a chair at the window, and slashed at her left wrist with a dagger-shaped shard of glass

A nurse heard the crash and arrived in time to prevent her bleeding to death.

By the time I was informed, she had already been transferred to the psychiatric unit.

That night, at home, I stared at the delayed transmission of humankind's first ever landing on another planet. I watched the silver-suited explorers venture out across the red sands of Mars, but for all the emotion the sight evoked in me they might have been cartoon figures in the latest Disney feature film.

***

The department at Laura's college gave her indefinite compassionate leave.

I sold the house quickly, at a loss, and bought a small place in a village closer to Oxford. Dan and a neighbour helped me move, and while I was visiting Laura they went through Ella's room, removing all her belongings and clothes. I told Dan what I wanted keeping of Ella's effects – few items of clothing, a teddy bear, some drawings – and they stored them in a sealed box which I placed in the attic of the new house, for the day when I would be strong enough to open it and use the contents as mnemonics, a part of the healing process.

I began painting again. I finished the commissions I had neglected – banged them out on auto-pilot with little regard as to their quality – and then started a series of paintings for myself.

They were dark, of course, and introspective, freighted with guilt and regret, containing self-referential symbols and icons known only to myself. They were not for general consumption. I might not even show Laura them. They were for the cowering, grief-stricken, guilt-ridden coward deep within me. They were a catharsis.

Ella came to me in dreams. Her face drifted into my vision, ethereal, ghost-like, and always she was wearing an accusing stare. Always, too, she asked me, "Why did you kill me, daddy?"

I would awake screaming, terribly alone in the empty bed.

***

Laura began slowly to emerge from her suicidal fugue. Heavily sedated, she responded to my visits. She talked to me. I told her about the new house, the garden, the studio – a converted stable at the bottom of the garden.

We never discussed Ella, or the accident. That would have been too painful.

Two months after my daughter's death, Laura was discharged. I drove her home in the second-hand Rover I had bought three weeks ago. She was quiet all the way, seemingly sedate. She was still on medication.

I showed her around the house, my studio, with my latest canvasses turned to the wall.

I left the bedroom until last. On the dresser I had placed a single photograph of Ella, smiling, filling the room with light and life.

Her glance took them in, quickly, but she made no comment.

Over dinner that evening, with a glass of French red wine, she told me that she was going back to work next week. I smiled, encouraged, buoyed by this evidence of her positivism and by half a bottle of merlot.

Only later, after a long silence, did she say, "Do you know what's the worst thing, Ed?"

Something plummeted within me. I shook my head.

She said, simply, "The future."

I let the silence stretch. At last I responded, "The future?"

"The future that's been denied us," she said calmly, and I wanted to cry out, tell her to stop.

She went on, relentless, "So much of our thoughts of the future were predicated by the fact of Ella. It was *all* about Ella. I planned ahead, imagining her at eight, at ten, at eighteen. I had a whole imaginary life charted, with you and me and her..." She was crying now, tears rolling down her cheeks. She shook her head. Her fingers tightened on her glass. She finished bitterly, "And now all that's gone, gone."

"Stop!"

She looked up at me. "You did the same?"

"Of course." What parent didn't? I had been battling against the absence of future certainties myself, over the weeks since the accident. We invest so much time in the paradoxical, imponderable fact of our children's futures that, when those futures are so cruelly torn away, we are left doubly bereft: consigned to a present filled with vast absence, to a future deficient of hope.

Laura flung her glass, contents and all, against the wall, then stood quickly, evading my attempt to stop her, pull her to me. She screamed, a wail I can hear to this day, and sobbing threw herself after the glass, battering herself against the walls in the corner of the room, back and forth, berserk, until I pulled her to me in a grip less compassionate than vicious with fear.

And held her, and rocked her, mouthing that I was sorry, sorry. What else could I say?

***

She returned to work, lecturing in Seventeenth Century English literature. I lost myself in my own work, spending long hours in the studio, absorbed. Laura talked about counselling, but I declined: I had my own form of therapy. She was seeing someone linked to her college, she told me, but I refrained from asking how it might be helping her.

She was still on sedation. She was not the Laura I had known and loved, the pre-accident Laura. She moved through life as if walking on cut glass, delicately, wincing from time to time. These were her good periods, when she somehow managed to hold her grief in check.

At other times, when she thought she could give full reign to her anguish without hurting me, I would come in from the studio to find her weeping, or wailing inconsolably.

My guilt was compounded by my inadequacy to say or do anything that might ease her pain.

Then, while I was painting one afternoon, she came in from work early, unannounced, and confronted me in the studio.

I had had no time to remove the canvas from the easel –

though she was so intent on unburdening herself that she only winced at what she saw in the painting, before saying, "Ed, we can't go on like this."

For a terrible second I thought that she was suggesting separation.

She went on, "We've got to see someone."

"I thought you were."

"A grief counsellor, for all the good it's done." She shook her head. "There's someone at college. He approached me the other day. He thinks he can help. Both of us."

"I don't need the help of psychiatrists. I can handle this myself."

She heard out my anger, staring at me with her calm blue eyes. "He's not a psychiatrist. He works in the neuroscience department – he's the chairman of a private IT company."

"Neuroscience? What are you suggesting? Lobotomy?"

My anger didn't faze her. She had a wonderful way of tolerating my idiocies. She said, "It's hard to explain, and I'm not sure I can do it full justice. I suggest we go and see him. Together."

I stared at her.

"Please, Ed. It might help."

I hesitated. "I don't want to share my pain with strangers!"

Her gaze was even. "You don't even want to share your pain with me," she said, gesturing to the dark images on the canvas behind me. "You don't even want to share your guilt with me."

She reached out, and I came into her arms, and said that yes, yes of course we should seek help.

That night I lay awake, thinking of Ella, of all the joy she gave us, and it came to me that there was no pain so great.

***

I'd met Laura ten years earlier, at an exhibition of my early work at her college. I was in my early thirties at the time, and trailing a string of failed relationships in my wake. I had no intention of getting seriously involved with anyone, not even a slim, beautiful, golden-haired woman in her late twenties, and then Laura walked up to me, wine glass in hand, and said how much she liked my paintings.

I overcame my initial inferiority complex: Laura Markham was a high-flying intellectual with a well-received book behind her, a dozen conference papers and a string of articles in learned academic journals – and I had left school at sixteen to paint.

Then I discovered that, despite her intimidating knowledge of Derrida and Lacan and post-colonial theory, she was an intimidated woman, unsure of her own worth, in need of love and affection. We were married a year later.

Would it be sexist and demeaning to say that, in my view, the birth of our daughter fulfilled Laura in a way that her profession never had? Perhaps not – for Ella fulfilled a need in me that even my painting had never managed.

***

Memories...

A host of pleasant memories sluiced though me as I accompanied Laura through the gates of her college, across the quadrangle, and into the maze of ancient corridors to the study of Professor James Enright.

He was surprisingly young. I put him at no older than forty. Tall, refined, very public-school – I imagined a cloistered life spent in academia, cosseted through a degree, a doctorate, post-doc fellowship, then a junior lectureship, followed by a series of promotions culminating in his present eminent position: Chair of Neuroscience, Oxford.

Perhaps the uneducated yob in me resented the idea that this effete scholar, with little knowledge of the outside world, thought he might be able to ease our pain.

Perhaps I should have been suitably grateful.

He sat behind his desk, somehow managing to appear tall even when seated, steepled his fingers and declaimed.

His voice was a plummy distillate of E.M Forster and

Betjeman. I told myself that he could no more help his accent than I could my Devonian burr – but he did sound patronising and elitist.

"I take it that Laura has appraised you of my latest work, Mr Carstairs?"

Laura said, "I thought I would let you explain the process."

Enright nodded. "In that case I might begin with a short overview of the theoretical base for my research, if I may?"

I stared at Laura. We'd come here for help, not a lecture.

Enright gave forth. Ninety per cent of what he said went straight over my head. He had the exasperating habit of talking through my questions. I've noticed this with some intellectuals: they have in common with autistics the inability to appreciate the other person's point of view, and hurriedly say, "Yes, yes..." waiting for the first opportunity to jump back into their own solipsistic riff.

I'll paraphrase what I did understand of his speech.

"We are coming to understand more and more the working of the brain," Enright said. "My company, Neuro-tech, has refined our research and located the source of memories within the thalamus, the hippocampus and the temporal lobe cortex. More, we can actually tag specific memories. My team has developed the process of selecting target memories and effectively initiating their subsequent extirpation."

I squeezed my eyes shut. When I opened them I stared at Enright and said, "In other words, you can edit memories?"

He inclined his head. "Put crudely, yes, we can. We call the process Mem-erase."

"So you could... you could edit from our memories the day of the accident, the accident itself?"

Enright assented, a slight smile playing on his lips. Perhaps he was human, after all?

Or, as I was to think later, perhaps he was inhuman?

Laura leaned forward, eagerly, and gripped my arm. "Don't you see, Ed, the horror of what happened, the accident... we could be rid of it for ever."

I sat back, aware of my thumping heart. How many times had I woken in the dark early hours from nightmares of the accident, haunted by the visions of my daughter lying crushed beneath the back wheels of the Volvo?

"As easy as that?" I said. "Zap, and they're gone? What about our... how to put it? Our memories of the memory? What about all the times since the accident that I've relived what happened? Christ, not an hour passes..." I stopped, aware of the catch in my throat.

Enright said, "For the process to be one hundred percent effective, Mr Carstairs, it would be necessary for the entire corpus, as it were, of your memories of your daughter to be expunged from your consciousness."

I opened my mouth to say something, but words were beyond me. I turned and looked at Laura. She had the good grace to look away.

To Laura I said, "Are you serious? You want to... to effectively get rid of Ella. Wipe her completely from our memories?"

She had obviously considered my objections. "Ed, Ella is already wiped from our futures... For our sanity, we could lose the memories."

I held up a hand. "Lose the memories'? Isn't that a euphemism? You actually mean that we'd lose our daughter."

She grimaced. "We *have* lost her, damn you!" she cried.

I shook my head. "I can't think about a future without the memories, the recollections of the good times. They mean something to me, Laura. They were the happiest times I've ever..." I stopped again, unable to continue for fear of breaking down.

I turned to Professor Enright. "Thank you for your consideration. I couldn't begin to consider taking up your offer. I can't speak for my wife." I left it at that, anger in my tone, stood and hurried from the room.

I paced the plush, carpeted corridor, stared down upon by a phalanx of stern-faced Deans portrayed inexpertly in oil and acrylic.

Laura joined me minutes later.

She murmured, “I had to excuse your rude behaviour,” as we fell into step and hurried from the college.

I kept my rage in check.

“I don’t see how you could even contemplate...” I began, and sneered, “Mem-erase indeed!”

We were silent for the duration of the drive home. Once there I sought sanctuary in my studio and resumed work. I lost myself in the depiction of tortured figures, dark little-girl-shapes consigned to oblivion...

Laura was silent during dinner. She drank with a forced determination. As soon as I’d finished, I pushed back my chair and said that I intended to continue work.

She stood and followed me from the dining room, through the kitchen. She stood in the doorway as I crossed the cobbled yard. “Don’t you ever think of me?” she said.

I stopped and stared at her. “What did you say?”

“What the hell,” she said, biting off each word with barely suppressed anger, “what the hell do you think it was like for me? I was standing there, watching, unable to do... to do a damned thing. *I saw it all*!”

I was torn, I admit, between striking Laura and attempting to embrace and comfort her. Instead of doing either, I said, “And what the hell do you think it was like for me? Spare a thought for me, Laura. How do you think I feel, knowing that I was responsible for... that I...” I took a breath. “I have it on my conscience twenty-four hours a day! How wonderful, how fucking wonderful, it’d be for me to simply wipe away the pain! But I’m not doing that – I’m not taking the cowardly, easy option, if it means losing the only things I have that allow Ella to remain alive – my memories of her!” Tears rolling down my cheeks now, I stumbled off to the studio, cursing, raging, and found my stash of brandy and sought oblivion in the only way I knew how.

***

Laura was sleeping when I eventually came to bed, and she went to work early the following morning. I spent a bad day, plagued by the memories of the accident. I tried to paint, but even this catharsis failed me. I even hit the bottle again, and then was overcome by inordinate guilt at seeking solace in the stultifying balm of alcohol. I hurled the bottle across the studio and faced my demons sober.

I considered everything Professor Enright had said, and thought through the consequences. What if I did accede, and had all memories of Ella expunged from my consciousness – how easy, how pain-free, that would be.

And how corrupt.

We are, as human beings, the sum of our experiences, and little else. The wonder of maturity is the realisation we all come to, sooner or later: that we have learned, or failed to learn, from our mistakes, that we are the people we are because of the decision we have made, whether those decisions were for good or bad. Our memories, often false or faulty, are the only indices of our experiences, and without these indices we are incomplete.

How could I remain true to my humanity, to the artist I claimed to be, if I had Ella eradicated from my awareness?

How could I be true to the love of my daughter? I owed it to her brief existence to exalt it in the only way I knew how – in my memory.

That night Laura was silent during dinner, and I fully expected another argument.

Over coffee she broached the subject.

"I've been thinking it over, Ed."

I winced. I prayed that she would not accede to Enright's treatment. I nodded. "And?"

She took a breath. "If I don't have the Mem-erase therapy, then will you at least allow me to remove the photos of Ella from the bedroom?"

I felt like telling her that she should work to come to some accommodation with the painful reminders of the past – but that would have been churlish and small-minded of me.

I nodded. "That's fair enough," I said.

That night, when I entered the bedroom, all the photos I'd put on display over the weeks, the framed snaps of Ella at school, on the beach, in the local park, in my arms, hugging Laura, smiling, smiling, had been cleared away. There was no evidence in the house, now, that she had ever existed – save for my secret store of memorabilia in the attic, and the more copious store of memories in the attic of my head.

***

Life continued.

The Mars mission successfully erected the dozen living-domes, awaiting the arrival of the multi-national colony *en route* from Earth – but I found myself unable to concentrate on what before might have fascinated me.

Laura threw herself into her work. Exam term came and she was stressed and overworked, as usual. She put in long hours, and I often ate dinner alone. I, for my part, worked through the series of cathartic oils depicting my abstracted nightmares. I had bad days, and even on good days I had bad hours of debilitating remorse, but I was coming to some acceptance of what had happened, some accommodation of the magnitude of our devastating loss.

As the weeks passed, it came to me that Laura was working through her loss, too. At lest, she cried less in my company – though she might have sought privacy in which to wail: the mantle of melancholy, which had been ever-present, lifted from her demeanour. She laughed a little, from time to time; she reached out for me, voluntarily, which she had ceased to do after the accident.

We made love for the first time since after Ella's death, six months earlier, and it was a wondrous sharing of what before we had taken for granted, an affirmation of our love and a token of hope.

After one afternoon in bed, as the sun cascaded into the room and warmed us, I said, "Remember when Ella –"

Laura's vision clouded suddenly, and she said, "Please, Ed..."

Chastened, aware that perhaps I was further along the road to recovery than was Laura, I nodded and held her to me.

In time, in time...

***

I looked about for new subjects, and decided I wanted to paint nudes. I asked Laura to pose, but she declined, as I thought she might. I hired a model from Oxford and she came twice a week to my studio, and I embarked on a series of positive, life-enhancing studies.

Samantha was twenty-two, slim, blonde and I suppose attractive – though the reason I chose her from the three others who applied was because I found her face, her body, her *shape*, interesting. Only later, as I got to know her, did I wonder how much my choice had been influenced by the subconscious realisation that Samantha physically resembled the woman Ella might have become.

Weeks passed and Samantha and I developed a rapport, an understanding, that sometimes grows between artist and model. I explored her visually, getting to know every curve and sinew of her body, and of course I ta lked to her and got to know the person within the form I was portraying.

In time she came to represent to me the grown up daughter I now would never know. Certainly, as the weeks passed, I began to feel towards Sam what I had experienced before only in my relationship with Ella: a consuming paternal affection, a concern for her well-being.

This misplaced identification with Sam culminated one Saturday morning when I was in the studio with her. She was reclining on a settee, staring at me, holding her pose, while I painted.

I happened to look up from the canvas, into her eyes, and something in her regard, the innocent fixity of her stare, felled me.

She was Ella, and yet not Ella, and in that second I was

flooded with despair, the terrible knowledge, almost made incarnate, of what I had lost – of what I had destroyed.

I sobbed, fell to my knees and sobbed.

Sam uncurled from her pose and hurried across the studio. Naked, she knelt before me, reached out and took me in her arms. I am convinced that there was no sexual intent in the gesture, just the desire to console. I held onto her and wept.

A little later she stiffened in my arms, and at the same time I heard the studio door creak open. I turned, still embracing Sam, to see Laura framed in the doorway, a realist study in shock.

Before I could say a word she gave an abbreviated cry and ran from the studio.

Sam said, "Ed, I'm sorry. I –"

"I know. Don't worry."

I stood and hurried outside. By the time I emerged into the dazzling sunlight, momentarily blinded by the sudden brightness, Laura had climbed into her car.

She reversed down the drive, crunching gravel. I flinched and called her name, but she was already on the main road and accelerating away.

Sickened, I returned to the studio. Sam was dressing hurriedly, embarrassed. "I'm sorry."

"Sam, I understand. I'll talk to Laura. It'll be okay."

She gave me a faint smile as she swept past me and left the studio.

I stood there for a long while, regarding the half finished painting of Ella as she might have been.

Then I found the brandy and drank.

***

It was dark, after ten, by the time Laura returned home.

I was still in the studio, pretty much drunk by then. I heard the car come to a halt in the drive, the door open and shut and Laura walk towards the back door. I gave her five minutes, then stood unsteadily and followed her inside.

Between bouts of self-pity, and raging grief, in more lucid moments, I had rehearsed an apology, an explanation of what had happened in the studio that morning.

"Laura..." I found her in the bedroom, readying herself for bed.

She looked up and smiled. "Ed, you're late. How was work?"

The bright tone of her enquiry disconcerted me. She was not being sarcastic. I stood in the doorway and swayed, blinking drunkenly at her, thinking that my senses must be at fault.

"Are you coming to bed, Ed?"

"About this morning – I want to explain."

She smiled at me, as if she didn't know what I was talking about. "About what?"

"Samantha, it wasn't what you think."

"Oh, Samantha. Your model."

"I just wanted to say..." But under the light of her smile, I could not continue.

She said, "Will you stop swaying like a drunk and come to bed!"

I was too drunk, too confused, to make sense of what was happening. I undressed and rolled into bed, and Laura pressed herself to me.

She was passionate. We made love. I recall her energy, my retarded reactions, and something else. At some point while entangled and sweating I recall thinking that I was making love to a stranger.

Laura made no reference to the incident with Sam the following morning, or that evening. It was as if it had never happened. I awoke with a pounding migraine, with only a hazy recollection of what had occurred the day before, my breakdown in front of Sam, Laura's odd behaviour the night before.

Later, I wondered how I could have been so blind. But I had been drunk, and confused, and unhappy, and I did not make the connection.

The truth hit me on the Monday evening when Laura returned home from college.

***

She was working in her study and I was preparing dinner. We had three bottles of red wine to choose from, and I made my way along the corridor to the study to ask which she might prefer. I opened the door and looked in; Laura was reading a sheet of paper, and as I stepped into the room she hurriedly hid it beneath a book and smiled brightly at me.

"Ed?"

"Ah... I was wondering which wine you'd like?"

"The Gallo will be fine."

I returned to the kitchen, wondering what she had been reading. We had a trusting relationship: I had no secrets from my wife – no pieces of paper that I would be loath to show her – and I liked to think that neither did she.

The jealous fool in me was piqued.

I heard the study door open and close, and seconds later the bathroom door. I made my way to the study, slipped inside and regarded her desk.

The corner of the paper she had been reading protruded from beneath a Penguin Freud.

I pulled it out and began reading.

I had to sit down. I collapsed into the chair and a hot flush rushed through me, making me suddenly nauseous.

The writing was in Laura's neat, bold hand

I had a daughter called Ella. She was five. She died in an accident. Ed accidentally reversed the car over her. I witnessed the accident. I've removed all her photos. Ed refused James' help – so he's still living with the guilt. That's why he's so depressed so much of the time. When he wants to talk about it, I refuse. I know it's hard on Ed, but he did spurn Mem-erase, after all.

There was more, but I heard the toilet flushing; I replaced the paper and hurried from the study.

I returned to the kitchen. I busied myself at the stove. My hands were shaking. I felt angry. Angry enough to hit out, to hurt. I was consumed with rage.

I tried to control my anger, so that when I confronted Laura with what she had done I would be rational, reasonable.

She entered the room; I should say *breezed* into the room, cheerful, smiling.

Why had I been so blind? How had I failed to notice her bonhomie, her blithe high spirits? Hers had not been the demeanour of a woman suffering the loss of a daughter.

She took her place at the table. I served the meal. I sat opposite her, sickened by the sight of the food before me, by Laura's bright smile across the table.

She ate. She poured two generous measures of wine.

I said, "I've been thinking about Ella."

She winced. "Ed, you know –"

"What? I know how you don't like thinking about her?" I said with more bitterness than I intended. "But we had a beautiful daughter, Laura; she was our life. She fulfilled us. She made the future something wondrous, to be cherished. And then she was gone, just like that, in a terrible , meaningless, stupid accident."

Laura stared at her plate, her mouth held oddly, off-centre, stalled mid-chew, an expression almost forbearing, or perhaps guilty?

I went on, "I've been thinking as well about that day we went to see Professor Enright, and what he offered us, and I've been thinking –" my hands were shaking, and my voice wavered "– been thinking about how inhuman that offer was, don't you think? I mean, I mean... grief is a process that has to be lived through, Laura. There's no easy option. You just can't sweep it under the carpet, forget the accident ever happened. Also," I said, near to tears now, "also, Laura, we owe it to Ella, too. I mean... I mean, I couldn't just let her go. My memories are all I've got of her."

I stopped. I stared across the table, into my wife's comprehending eyes.

I said, "How could you?" in barely a whisper.

She said, "Ed..." a breath freighted with the desire to be understood.

"How could you wipe our daughter from your memory?"

"Ed, you don't understand. You can't comprehend the pain I was going through."

I hung my head and wept. I was overcome by her treachery.

I looked up and said, "Can't I? Don't you think I suffered, still am suffering?"

"Ed, I saw it happen. I witnessed the horror and there was nothing I could do."

And, although she spoke the words, there was a vital weight of emotion absent from them. They sounded like an editorial, summarising how she *should* have felt.

I stared at her. "I lived through it as well, for Chrissake! I'm still living through it! It's the only way. The only way we can come to some understanding is to feel the pain and accept –"

"Ed, Ed... But why? Why is all the pain necessary? Why torture yourself?" She stopped, a light of understanding in her eyes. "It's the guilt, isn't it? You've burdened yourself with all the guilt and in a bid to punish yourself, you refused the treatment?"

"No!" I said, but at the same time, consumed by self-doubt, a part of me wondered if she were right.

"It's a betrayal of Ella," I said. "We owe it to her to remember the good times."

Laura held my gaze. She said, "Ella is no longer part of our futures. I saw no reason not to have her expunged from my past, too. Of course I knew I had a daughter, and I can appreciate the pain I must have felt, but I'm free of it now, and grateful."

I shook my head and whispered, "We can't live like that. Pain is part of the experience of being alive. How can we claim to be fully alive if we simply wipe pain from our lives every time we don't like what we've experienced?" I stopped, understanding hitting me.

"The other day, when you entered the studio and saw me holding Sam. Your lack of reaction that night... You had it wiped, didn't you? Rather than learn the truth, you ran off and had it Mem-erased!"

She smiled at me, but the smile was faltering. "What was the truth, Ed?"

I waved. "Would you believe me, anyway? I was painting Sam, and she reminded me of Ella – how Ella might have been – and I lost it. Broke down. Sam tried to comfort me. You came in and saw us..."

"Well, I no doubt thought at the time that I couldn't live with the knowledge of what you were doing."

"So you conveniently had it wiped?"

"Sometimes, Ed, you deal with pain in the only way you know how."

I drank my wine. We sat in mutual, hostile silence. I said at last, "You have no idea how wonderful a little girl Ella was."

Laura got up and hurried from the room.

I sat in the descending twilight for a long time, drinking.

***

I did not mention Mem-erase again. I tried to act as though nothing at all had come between us. Outwardly we continued as we had for weeks and months and years: Laura went out to work while I painted and prepared the evening meal, which we would eat while chatting amiably of nothing in particular, whiling away the evening with red wine and a film.

But we could no longer connect.

She no longer had the experience of our daughter's life, or death. She did not know what I was going through – how my grief informed my every word and action – and I could not comprehend the grief-free, care-free world which Laura now inhabited.

One of the wonders of marriage is that shared experience brings greater understanding of one's partner: the past is a storehouse of mutual emotions from which to draw strength and comfort.

We were denied that experiential storehouse: now Laura looked at life from a vantage point I could not reach, and inevitably we grew apart.

***

One month later we had friends up from London for the weekend. Dave and Sophie DeVere were both artists, Dave an abstract painter and Sophie a sculptor, whom I had met at art college fifteen years earlier. Dave was perhaps my closest friend, and on their first meeting Laura and Sophie had hit it off like reunited sisters.

We had not seen them since the accident, and I suppose the meeting might have been fraught with potential awkwardness on both sides. However, I defused that when I greeted them, putting on a show of exaggerated bonhomie and chatting away about my current work, their respective projects and art in general.

They had a daughter, a year older than Ella had been. They had left her in London. They didn't even mention her.

The weekend went well, even if Laura was somewhat withdrawn and quiet.

On the Sunday afternoon, before they were due to leave, we went on a long walk through the summer countryside. At one point Sophie fell into step with me and increased her pace, putting distance between Dave and my wife.

"Ed..." Sophie began. I glanced at her. She was pulling a querulous moue.

"Mmm?"

"I hope you don't mind my asking, but is Laura on medication?"

"No," I said. "No, she came off it a while ago."

"Oh... Only, it's just... Well, I hope you don't mind me saying, but she seems –" She shook her head. "I know what you went through must have been sheer hell, but Laura seems... not the person she was." She reddened and quickly glanced at me. "I'm not putting this at all well, am I? What I mean is – I could always rely on Laura for sympathy, understanding. Last night I told her about Dave and me..." Dave had mentioned to me that their marriage had been going though a rocky patch lately. "Laura seemed, well, unconcerned. It was almost as if she couldn't understand what I was saying, or wasn't bothered. It wasn't at all like the old Laura."

I nodded. "Losing Ella has changed her," I said, and left it at that.

But what Sophie had said set alarm bells ringing – together with something that happened a few days later.

***

It was early evening; we had finished a meal and were in the lounge, reading. Laura looked up from her book and stared at the print hanging over the hearth.

"I don't like that painting," she said.

Something within me sank, deflated.

It was a big abstract reproduction by Bacon, which I adored. I'd bought it five years ago, a present to myself after a particularly important sale. Laura had told me in no uncertain terms that she hated it and didn't want it in the house, and we'd argued. Our disagreement was heated, and escalated into a shouting match. I accused Laura of selfishness – she had hung pieces around the place which I deplored – and Laura retaliated by saying that I was being insensitive. We hadn't spoken for days, until she had relented and allowed me to hang the print where I wanted. But the rancour had left a lasting, bitter taste.

"I hate it," she said now. "It makes me feel uneasy. Would you take it down?"

I stared at her. "We've had this argument before. You said that I could keep it."

Her expression clouded. "I did?"

I retreated into my book, heart racing.

***

Over the next couple of months I lost myself in my work. I retreated to the studio at every opportunity, and where before I had spent time with Laura in the house or the garden because I craved her company, now I sought solitude: to be with her was to remind myself how far away she was.

I no longer employed Sam as a model. I did not want to put

myself in a situation where I might weaken and seek comfort in her pity and compassion. I was tempted, for the terrible motive of exacting some kind of revenge on Laura, but thank God the moral being in me stayed my hand.

Nine months after Ella's death, I received a phone call from one of Laura's colleagues, a woman I'd met once or twice.

"Is Laura there?" she asked after the customary pleasantries.

"She's teaching today," I said.

An odd silence. Then, at last, "Oh..."

Uneasy, I said, "What?"

"Well, I'm not sure that it's my place to –"

"What is it?"

"Ed, I don't know how to tell you. Laura was suspended from her post a few weeks ago. I was just ringing to see how she was."

"Suspended? Why? I mean –"

"The standard of her teaching," she said. "Her ability to draw conclusions in her work, her lack of empathy with the students. The department thought it best to offer her extended leave."

All that day, until Laura returned, I thought through what the woman had told me.

Laura had left the house at nine every morning, as if nothing was wrong, maintaining the charade that she was still employed by the university.

I tried to determine which shocked me most: the fact that the university had suspended her, or her duplicity in not telling me and acting as if nothing untoward had occurred.

I cooked the evening meal as usual, opened a bottle of wine.

Laura came home and hurried straight to her study with hardly a greeting, this stranger my wife had become.

She would emerge later to share a quick meal with me, before going to bed early while I sat up and tried to read.

As we ate, I said, "You didn't tell me you were suspended."

She avoided my stare. "It was probably for the best. I couldn't concentrate. I need a little time to get my thoughts together."

I nodded. "So... where do you spend your days now?"

She regarded her half-empty wine glass. "I go over to the

library most days."

I stared at her. "You have absolutely no idea what you've done, have you?"

She looked up. "Pardon?"

"It's Mem-erase, isn't it? How much of your past have you had wiped?" I stared at her until she looked away. "It's changed you, Laura. You've lost the ability to... to connect."

She stood and strode to the door, then turned and said, "Go to hell, Ed! You don't know what it's like, living with you these days! You're always so damned depressing!"

***

A week later I came in from the studio to find Laura packing a suitcase. I stood in the doorway of the bedroom and watched her.

"Leaving?" I said, affecting casualness.

She looked up. "I've had enough of your silences, Ed. Your moods. I can't stand being around you any more. You're a little black hole, sucking in all my energy."

"I wonder why..." I said, more to myself.

Amazingly, I achieved a kind of objectivity as she told me this. A part of me was ripped asunder, while another, removed part of myself reminded me that this Laura was no longer the woman I had loved for over a decade.

She finished packing and hurried past me, and I said nothing and watched her go, filled with an emptiness very much like grief.

I slept in the spare room, not wanting to be reminded of the joy we had shared in the bedroom. She left a mess of clothes and possessions, which I did my best to straighten out and store away.

The following day, while tidying the bedroom, I came across a folder containing Laura's bank statements.

I sat down and leafed through them, and discovered that for the past four months, at fortnightly intervals, she had withdrawn regular amounts of a thousand euros.

I tried to paint, but found it impossible to concentrate. I was beset by waking nightmares. I thought about Laura's addiction to

Mem-erase, and where it might end.

She was systematically eradicating from her life all her experiences of pain, from major trauma like Ella's death to much lesser incidents of hurt. I extrapolated the consequences of her actions and was filled with horror at my conclusions.

As she removed from her life all memory of one pain, then surely her ability to deal with pain in general – to learn from experience and grow, adapt to the agony of being alive – would diminish, so that her capability to work though trauma would become a relative process: as each pain was eradicated, so the next lesser pain would rush in to fill the vacuum of her life and become just as agonising and unbearable, as she would have no experience of real pain against which to measure it. So she would have this pain removed, and so on and so on... in a terrible reductionist cycle that would carve away, bit by bit, all her past experience, culminating in the whittling down of her humanity until only an empty, emotionless zombie stood in place of the woman who had been my wife.

I attempted to get through to Professor Enright, but was informed that he was away on a week's holiday. I left my name and said that I would call back.

***

I attempted to find Laura and beg her to return. Life without her was hell. I wanted her back, even though she was not the woman I had married.

I contacted the university, her friends in town, but they had no idea where she was.

In the event, I found her quite by accident.

Unable to work, I walked into town one afternoon and decided to console myself in a quiet, olde worlde pub that served a blissful pint of Old Peculier.

I sat in the corner and drank, trying not to dwell on the future. The jukebox was playing something by the Eagles, and the twanging National guitar brought back memories of the days I had dated Laura.

I was on my third pint when I saw the woman across the room.

For a fraction of a second I had an objective view of her, as a stranger might have seen the woman: a straggle-haired, drawn-faced woman in her early forties, finding pathetic solace in a series of rum and blacks.

Then, with a sudden and wrenching realisation, I saw that it was Laura.

I picked up my pint and, to the plangent tones of a lead guitar solo, walked across to her.

Laura looked up. Almost winced.

I sat down across form her and said, "I'm missing you, Laura. Come back."

She was silent for a long time. She looked dreadful. She had once told me, near to tears, that she had reached the age where her appearance needed constant renovation in order that she appear – in her own words – presentable. I had said that she was talking rubbish, that she would always be beautiful to me.

Now I saw what she meant. She had let herself go. Her hair was lank and greasy, her skin pale. Without make up, she looked half dead.

She said, in barely a whisper, "Why should I come back?"

"We had so much," I began.

She screwed her eyes half-shut, as if to recall what we might have had together.

"Ed, it's true what... what someone said. Who was it? Anyway, they said that we're really only the aggregate of our experiences, and if we have no memory of those experiences... then we become nothing."

"Laura... how much have you had erased?"

She raised a smile at that. "Don't know. How could I? Maybe a lot. Whole areas of the past... they're gone." She smiled to herself.

I tried to take her hand on the table, but she pulled i away. "Laura. Come back. We can start again. It was wonderful, believe me."

"Ed... it wouldn't work. I don't understand you anymore. The worlds we inhabit are very different now."

"You mean, you're different," I said.

She stood up. "I'm so sorry."

"Don't go."

"I need the loo."

I watched her hurry along the warped timber passage. I stared at my pint, then drained it off and bought another.

I waited, and ten minutes must have elapsed before it dawned on me that she wasn't coming back. I walked down the corridor. There was a rear door, next to the entrance to the womens' toilet.

I returned to my pint and drank.

***

The following day, hungover, in desperation, I rang the college and tried to get through to Professor Enright. A receptionist informed me that he was not at college, but at the offices of Neuro-Tech, and gave me his number.

"Do you know what you've done?" I said when I was put through.

"Who is this?"

I explained who I was, and what his Mem-erase process had done to my wife.

"Mr Carstairs, I assure you that I conducted only one session of strategic Mem-erase with your wife, specifically to removed the terrible memory of her loss."

"You're lying!" I yelled, and catalogued the list of experiences removed from Laura's awareness.

"I'm sorry, but there is no way I can account for this. Please, if you'll allow me a little time to investigate the matter..."

I replaced the receiver, wondering at his words.

An hour later, the phone rang. "Mr Carstairs, Professor Enright here. I've been looking into the case of your wife's Mem-erase. I've uncovered certain, ah... shall we say, irregularities. If you would care to come over to Neuro-Tech and discuss the matter with me."

I set off immediately and thirty minutes later parked outside a low, ultra-modern, glass-fronted building on a new science park to the west of the city.

A uniformed receptionist with the lock-jaw smile of an air-hostess showed me along a carpeted corridor to a minimalist, white-walled office.

Enright sat behind a desk shaped like an arrowhead, backed by a sheet-glass window overlooking a chamber busy with bearded techie-types. His donnish air was at odds with the spartan IT ambience of the place.

He shook my hand, then sat back and steepled his fingers, a look of concern spread across his usually unflappable features.

"Mr Carstairs," he began, "I can fully appreciate your concern. It appears that, after the initial process of Mem-erase, your wife approached a junior research assistant and... this is where the irregularity occurred... paid the woman to conduct further – and might I say highly illegal – sessions to remove certain memories. Needless to say there will be a thorough investigation and the research assistant in question will be dismissed. There might even be grounds for criminal proceedings."

I heard him out. At last I said, "That's all very well, but the fact remains that my wife is, as you might imagine..." I went on to tell him of the person my wife had become.

He inclined his head. "I understand, but I can offer you hope."

I stared at him, hardly daring to ask, "You can?"

"The Mem-erase process is reversible, Mr Carstairs. What is taken away can be replaced. All memories are stored. I have located the files that contain your wife's missing life, as it were, and if she is willing then I see no reason why we cannot begin the restoration process immediately."

I thanked him, and told him that I would be in contact, and left Neuro-Tech filled with hope and, at the same time, despair: for what chance would there be of persuading the woman my wife had become of taking on the burden of pain she had paid to jettison in the first place?

***

I scoured Oxford for my wife. In increasing desperation I asked at every pub in the city, leaving photographs of Laura and my phone number in case she appeared.

I spent hours driving through the busy streets, staring out at the guarded faces of so many strangers. I was close to a nervous breakdown, strung out, drinking more and more and getting little sleep.

I had never really realised, while I'd had Ella and Laura, how much my happiness had been dependent on the people I loved.

One evening, as I was halfway down a bottle of Calvados, the phone rang.

I picked it up. "Yes?"

No reply.

"Who is it?"

Silence – and then I made out a voice. Small, frightened. A croak. "Ed."

"Christ, Laura? Is that Laura?"

"Ed, please help me."

"Where are you?"

"I need your help!"

"I'm here! I'm coming!"

She began weeping. "Oh, Christ... what have I done?"

"Laura?"

"I came so close, Ed. So close to... to having you wiped! I contacted them yesterday. You see, it seemed that the only thing that was making me unhappy was the memory of you. All those years... the good times together. Your love."

"Laura..."

"So I contacted Neuro-Tech. I wanted to wipe you. But they said... they told me that I couldn't, that they couldn't treat me."

"Laura, listen to me. I saw Enright the other day. He told me that the process was reversible."

"I know."

The silence rang. "You know?"

"They told me. They wanted me to come in." She paused, sobbing. "But, Ed, how can I have all the memories returned to me? I got rid of them for a reason, didn't I? How could I live through Ella's death again?"

I said, "It's the only way. It's the only way you can become the person you were."

"I need your help. I rang you because..."

"Laura?"

"I don't like the person I've become, Ed. But I'm not sure I'm strong enough to become the person I was."

"Where are you? I'll be right over."

She told me and, despite the drink blurring my vision, I hurried out into the cold October night and drove across town to the grubby suburb of student bed-sits and take-away food franchises.

I parked the car outside the address Laura had given me, hurried up a front path littered with empty pizza boxes and buckled take-away trays and rapped on the door.

A young woman answered. "Yes?"

Ignoring her, I looked around an untidy front room, then made for the stairs and climbed them despite the girl's protests. I came to a landing and counted three bedroom doors; two were open, the third closed. I approached the closed door and knocked.

Seconds later Laura said, "Ed?" and I almost wept with joy.

I pushed open the door, stepped inside and closed it behind me. A filthy room littered with old clothes and empty wine bottles...

Laura was sitting on the floor, the phone still cradled in her lap. Her eyes were swollen from crying, and she looked up at me with something like despair.

Then she said, "Ed?" in a tiny voice.

I stepped forward, reached out and pulled her to her feet. I held her. "There's something I want to show you," I gestured around the room. "Do you need to take –?" I began.

She shook her head. "There's nothing here I need."

We drove home in silence, Laura gripping my thigh all the way. From time to time she cried, and it was all I could do to stop myself from breaking down as I concentrated on the road.

At home I helped her from the car and walked her through the house. In the bedroom I sat her on the floor and said, "Wait there. I won't be a minute..."

Sniffing back her tears, she nodded, watching me with trusting, almost hopeful, eyes.

I found the step-ladders, removed the trap-door to the attic and reached inside.

I carried the box back to the bedroom and sat down beside my wife.

"What is it?"

"After the accident," I said, "while you were still in hospital, I saved a few things belonging to..."

I opened the box with clumsy, trembling fingers, and the sight of what was inside drew a painful sob from deep within me.

"This was Ella's favourite teddy," I said, lifting it out and handing it to Laura. "Mr Ted." I withdrew a dress and held it to my face, and the redolence of my dead daughter haunted me like a ghost. "And these are some drawings she made." I lifted them from the box and passed them to Laura.

Two crude stick figures on a line of green grass, with a big yellow sun in the sky and the words Mummy and Daddy in clumsy stick-writing underneath.

Laura said, "How will I cope, if I couldn't the first time?"

"You'll have me," I said. "We'll cope together."

She nodded, and reached out to me, and said, "Then, yes, of course. I love you, Ed."

***

Three months later we sat in the bedroom and I held Laura as she wept. Over the long weeks she had had her past returned, and today we had left the Neuro-Tech clinic for the very last time.

Around us were the reminders of our daughter: photographs

on the wall beside her stick-drawings; Mr Ted on the dresser, watching us.

Laura clung to me and wailed. “It’s so terrible!” she cried. “She was only five! My daughter! Ella...”

I wept with her. “I’m sorry. Laura, I’m so sorry.”

“*We’ve lost our daughter!*”

I held my wife. Together we relived the terrible moment of the accident, and we grieved.

Radio Trauma

Richard Wright

John sat in the darkness of the studio, waiting to be invited into thousands of homes across the country like some audio vampire. Pushing fingers into his forehead, he rotated them gently as his jingle kicked in. He had a headache, and it hurt to listen. In the producer's box, a small, enclosed booth at the far side of the studio, Miles hummed to himself. Only John heard him, as late night listeners whistled along to the jangling beat in their homes, ready to be wound up and set in motion.

"*This is a warning. You are entering the John Brosnan Zone. This is a warning. If you are of a nervous disposition, turn off your radio now. Your co-operation is appreciated. If your phone's there, you know the number. Pick up and share your wisdom with the nation. This is the John Brosnan show, and he's nothing without you.*"

John took a deep breath, ignoring the knitting needle stabbings in his temple, and introduced himself to a too willing nation.

"Of course, often I'm nothing *with* you, but tonight you're going to surprise me. I feel it in my tissues." That was a shameless lie. He could predict, almost to the call, what he was going to have to endure over the next few hours.

"No prizes for guessing the top subject tonight," he continued, "you've all seen the headlines. Horror author Christie Shelby was found dead in her London flat this afternoon. The police are being surprisingly cagey about the cause of death. You remember Christie, don't you?" John felt none of the venom that dropped from his lips. Just for once, he wished somebody would challenge the incendiary nonsense he whispered over the airwaves ever night. "She writes books so *scary*, you'll lose your mind if you read them."

It was a bold, tabloid statement, and Miles raised his eyebrows through the glass fronting of the producer's box.

"Okay," he amended, "most of us wouldn't. We all know there are those among us not best described as stable, though, don't we? We see them on Jerry Springer every day. Shelby set them on *fire*, guys. You all remember little Rebecca McKinley and the others. Can the killer be blamed for the shattering of his own sanity, or should Shelby take the blame for fuelling that particular blaze? We've had the discussion before, but does her death change your views? She'll never get another right of reply, so should we mourn her, or wipe our brows in relief?" John let the question hang. Earlier, he and Miles had argued the merits of hashing over the Shelby affair on air, but it had been front page news for the last year, ever since the murders began. Each of the six deaths was identical to key scenes from Shelby's potboilers, grisly page-turners with one-word titles like *Scar,* and *Claustrophobia.* Rebecca McKinley. Craig Fuller. Mark Lancaster. Olivia Johnson. George Williams. Samantha Burkett. McKinley was the worst. Twelve years old, for God's sake. The public adored that sort of thing. It was Jamie Bulger all over again, and ideal fuel for talk show hosts like John, and tabloid journalists the nation over.

Shelby had been categorically cleared of the murders, despite many of them occurring near her home. With no suspect in custody to analyse from afar, Shelby and her books were the next best target. There had even been protests outside her home, and she had barely stepped outside her front door for the last three months.

John knew better. Books didn't turn people into killers. Shelby had been persecuted for nothing, and he had been part of making that happen. Swallowing, he massaged his temples. It didn't matter. Whipping up the great unwashed was how he made his money, and these recent bouts of conscience helped nobody at all. "The floor's yours folks." Time to get started. "How's the switchboard looking Miles?"

"Since you name dropped your favourite author? Like Oxford Street at Christmas."

John gave a sigh so theatrical that Gielgud would have applauded. "Predictable, aren't they? Who's on line one? Hello?"

"Hello?" A woman, middle aged from the sound of it. Nervous, but determined. He liked to picture who he was speaking to.

"Hello."

"Hello?'"

John rolled his eyes. "*Hello*."

"Oh! Hello. I'd like to talk to John Brosnan please?" John sighed, his finger hovering over his keyboard, and the button that would disconnect her call. The night was off to a typical start. The great unwashed were on their usual form. "Right. I see. Can I ask what about?"

"I'd rather wait to tell John, if that's okay?"

"A private thought you'll only share with our host and nearly two and a half million listeners?"

"Sorry?" She was beginning to realise that something odd was happening. "Look, are you going to put me through to John?"

"Actually, he's just popped out. Can I take a message?"

"Popped out?"

"Popped, as you correctly say, out."

"Oh. I see. Can you tell him that Mary from Grimsby called to say that Christie Shelby was evil, and I'm glad she's dead, and I hope she's being sodomised by Hitler in hell."

John's eyes widened, and he smiled. Mary had some character after all. "Will do." He punched his finger down, cutting her off. "Some nights I could just cry. Let's go to line two. Gary from Liverpool, you're up."

"John! *Brilliant*!" Great. A scouser, probably somewhere in his late twenties, and vastly overexcited by what was almost certainly going to be no more than fifteen seconds of fame. "Hey, I'm a first time caller you know," John gritted his teeth. Every second caller wanted to tell him that, as though it would buy them some leniency on the matter of their imminent idiocy, "and I just wanted to tell you your show's *brilliant*, you know? Those books are sick man, but you got her where it hurts. *Brilliant*! I also wanted to know if your television show's coming back, because that was *absolutely* –"

John punched his finger down. "Brilliant. Yes, I think we've established that. I'll tell you what Gary, you pack your tongue away, and I'll try to dry the seat of my jeans. Miles, could you go over to the window?" Miles was barely paying attention, but he was long practised at being John's stooge. "That's right. Now have a quick look out and up. Good. It's a full moon isn't it?"

"Certainly is."

"What have I told you about full moon nights, Miles?"

Miles paused, his brain catching up with what he had been asked. "You said to cancel them."

"That's right, I did, didn't I? Cross your fingers and hope the next caller's from somewhere deep underground, far from the touch of the moon's gravity. On line four we have Keith. What's up, Keith?"

"Oh, hello Mr Brosnan. How are you?" A hard one to judge. The voice was cold and flat, with a very subtle softness that might once have been an Edinburgh lilt. John felt his hopes lift slightly at the hint of bored intelligence the voice conveyed. Perhaps he might even be able to engage in a conversation worth having. Stranger things had happened.

"Fading fast. Where you from Keith?"

"I can't tell you that. You would be able to find me."

Hopes of intelligent debate flushed away. John was long overdue a daytime show. The freaks mostly came out at night. "Think I'll be leading the villagers to your gate with a burning brand? Well, let's see, shall we? What's your problem?"

"You're really going to let me say? Without cutting me off, and making it sound like I've hung up?"

John's finger lingered above the keyboard, ready to do just that. "Entertain me, and we'll see."

"I want to start by saying that I'm a long time listener."

"Spare us."

"I just want everybody to know that I've been listening to you since you started, Mr Brosnan, so I know what I'm talking about."

"We'll take it as read."

"As you please. My point, then. I don't think you're a very nice person. You're in the wrong place. You set yourself above your listeners. You believe yourself superior to them. You have no respect for people, and that's what I'm here to help you see."

John chuckled for the microphone, not feeling the mirth, feeling only tiredness swamping through him. "Well, I hate to stand in the way of your Christian duty to improve me, but you've committed the cardinal sin of boring me, so I'm afraid..."

Somebody screamed into the telephone, high, long, and agonised, and John snatched the headphones away from his head with a gasp. Almost immediately, he cupped one speaker back to his left ear, needing to hear what was happening. "What? Keith..." Underneath the scream, which had strength in it yet, there was a second sound, a rhythmic, damp, grating, like somebody raking over wet gravel. John couldn't think of what to say, could only stare at Keith's flickering name on his monitor, his mouth open.

In the booth, there was a flurry of movement. Miles had caught up with events faster than John. "Jesus, I'll trace the call back and send an ambulance."

It was a lead that John could follow. "Keith?" The grating had stopped, and the scream lessened, hitching and whimpering as it sought new breath to continue. "What's happening there? Are you all right?"

"Yes, I'm all right." Keith's voice was calm and unflustered. In the background, the whimpering continued. There was somebody else there. When John was nine, he had owned a retriever called Tanya, who was mowed down by a car right in front of him. John had stayed with her while she died, a crowd forming around them both. Tanya had whined just like that until she had stopped breathing.

Somebody was making that noise right now, and it wasn't Keith.

Something was very wrong. The studio seemed to darken.

"What… what the *hell* just happened Keith? Are you fucking us around?"

"Dear me, no."

"Then…"

"Oh, *that.* I just severed my wife's right thumb with a hacksaw."

"What?" John shook his head. "You're stamping all over good taste, here my friend…" *Please*, John thought, as his bad feelings grew stronger. *Please let him be stamping all over good taste.*

"Perhaps you should speak to my wife. Tell him Sandy. Sandy?" A hard smack. Flesh on flesh.

"Hand…" She could barely speak, though the suddenness of her voice at the receiver was shocking enough in its implications. Her breath came in ragged gulps. She was English, but beyond that her accent was smothered with pain. "Cut my hand… bleeding…"

"That's fine, dear. I'm sure he has the idea. Do you have the idea, Mr Brosnan?"

John couldn't speak.

"I think he's for real, man." Miles was leaning in to the window dividing them, his fingers scissoring frantically. He was going to cut Keith off. They couldn't let this run live.

John tried to breathe normally, his skin cooling as he tried to remember what would happen next. When they cut the call, he would keep talking, pretend they were still broadcasting. It was a procedure they had agreed long ago, in anticipation of the suicidal calling to end their lives on air. Miles would switch the real broadcast back to the opening jingle, letting it loop over until another presenter could take over from a different studio, and giving John time to stall the caller until the line could be traced, and the police informed.

He took a breath. "Okay… okay Keith, let's all stay calm while we talk this –" He saw Miles switch the outgoing feed, and relief washed over him. If he screwed this up, he didn't want to do so in full public view. " – whatever you want, you can have it, okay? Just don't hurt her again, okay?"

"Give me the ear of the nation, Mr Brosnan. That's all I want."

"Well, you have it." John tried not to think of how untrue that was, in case it carried in his voice. "What do you want to tell them?" In the background, John heard music.

"One moment, Mr Brosnan. I have to check something."

Ice flooded John's chest. The music he was listening to was his own jingle beginning, and he was hearing it not from the producer's booth, but through his headset.

There was a ten second delay on the outgoing feed, so that any libellous statements or too foul language could be censored. Ten seconds ago, Miles had shoved the jingle on, disconnecting Keith from the very thing he wanted.

"Keith," he asked, tentatively. "Keith, are you there?"

There was another scream, sanity wrenching in its pain. John cried out in panic and sympathy. Miles was a blur of movement in the booth.

Sandy's howl became the world. John knew he was shouting into the microphone, but had no idea what he was saying. Miles vanished. His monitor faded to nothing. He was alone in a dark room. In that blackness, a woman was being brutally tortured in front of him, and there was nothing he could do about it.

Miles was twirling his fingers around and around, and John felt stupid for not understanding what he was trying to say.

The scream guttered out, and he could think again. Miles was telling him they were going back on air. John looked at his screen, and saw that they were broadcasting.

"We're on air! Keith, we're back on air! *Keith*!" Sandy's sobbing was weak. John was almost relieved. That showed she was alive, and nothing in that scream had suggested she would be.

"It's all right, Mr Brosnan, I can hear you. I should have mentioned that I have a radio on in the other room. I'll know if you try anything to stop me being heard. I *will* make my opinions known, Mr Brosnan."

"Yes. God yes, whatever you want." In that moment, he meant it. "Is she… is Sandy… okay?"

Keith tutted. "No John, she isn't. You've now caused me to remove a second finger from her right hand. I'm afraid she might never pen another letter. Also, she's probably bleeding to death. I don't suppose you have any idea how to tie a tourniquet?"

John struggled for words. "How to…"

Miles saved him. "John, stay with us, man. Look Keith, I'll keep you on air as long as you don't touch Sandy again, but she's going to be no kind of incentive if she's dead, is she? You got any bandages there?" Somehow, Miles achieved a calm, authoritative tone that John had never heard from him before.

"I may have Miles. As ever, you're a voice of reason in that studio. I'll be back in a minute. In the meantime, talk to Sandy. She could probably use a reassuring voice."

"No problem. No problem at all. We'll be right here when you get back."

"Yes. I'll kill my wife if you're not. Sandy, sweetheart? There's a man wants to talk to you."

"Sandy, you there?"

John wanted to join in, but his mouth wouldn't work. He tried to picture what Sandy looked like. Did she have blonde hair, or was she brunette? Was she pretty? All he could see in his mind were two severed fingers, lying on a linoleum floor.

"…here…"

"Listen, you're going to be fine, okay? We're going to sort this."

"…'kay…" Was she even hearing what Miles was saying? He doubted it.

"You're feeling shit, but don't freak out. You're in shock, that's all."

"…Keith…"

"I don't think Keith's feeling too great himself, but we'll help him Sandy. Okay? But we have to help you first, yeah? Has Keith taken the saw with him?"

"…saw… sore…"

"I know it hurts, but you have to tell me if he took the saw with him."

"Took the saw. The gun."

John swallowed his sudden nausea. "Oh Jesus, he's got a *gun…*"

"John, will you shut up! Sandy, which room did he go to?"

"…bathroom…"

"Is that an upstairs bathroom, Sandy?" Why all the questions? Miles was up to something, and John started to shake his head nervously.

"…upstairs…"

"Can you see the front door, Sandy? Are you near the front door?" John understood what was about to happen, and fear paralysed him. How long would Keith be gone?

"…uh huh…"

"Go for it. When you get to the street, scream your lungs out, yeah?"

"…Keith…"

"Hey, don't you be worrying about Keith. He's got me and John looking out for him? Right John?"

John wanted to stop this, to let Keith have what he wanted, but Miles was in control, and that meant the consequences were his problem. "Uh. Sure."

"See?"

"Oh. Okay." She could barely think, and Miles was using that to try to get her out. If she couldn't question, she would do what she was told.

There was a tap as she rested the telephone receiver on something solid. John wondered if she was moving at all, or just standing there, looking at her ruined hand with tears of pain and confusion leaking down her face.

"Sandy?" Keith, still distant, but clearly on the way.

"Sandy!" Desperation sharpened Miles's tone.

John gripped the table. She couldn't be caught. Not live on air. "Run, woman," he yelled.

Footsteps, moving at a fast trot on a hard surface.

Not linoleum, then. Probably a wooden floor.

John shook his head, trying to think of something to say that could stop what would happen next.

There was a sharp slap, and even in the distance it made John wince. A second thud, Sandy hitting that wooden floor, was followed by delirious whimpering. John's lips moved, but nothing useful came out. "Oh God. Oh God."

"Keith? You there? What are you doing?" Miles was pacing in the booth, unable to stand still as he spoke. "It was my fault, you hear that? I made her go. Keith?"

"Didn't I tell you I had a radio in the other room, Miles?"

"Yeah, you did. Look, I'm sorry, just don't –"

"I'll take no action this time for just one reason. I believe that you, Miles, had her best interests at heart. I think you actually see her as a human being. You aren't like Mr Brosnan. You deserve to be working with someone better."

Despite everything, John felt an absurd sense of shame. "*What?* What do you..." A nasty idea popped into his head. "Is that was this is about?" Was the man that badly severed from reality. "How I treat my callers?"

"That simplifies the matter, Mr Brosnan, but it is accurate as far as it goes."

Now that John was speaking, he couldn't stop. Somehow, he had to take control of the situation, and as he always did when under pressure, he let his mouth buy his brain some time. "Then Keith, you've got it all wrong. My callers are what my job is all *about.* I have nothing but respect for the people who pick up the phone and ring in."

"Respect? I'm surprised you don't choke on the word."

"No, no – that's not fair. You're... you're getting the job mixed up with the man. Don't you understand? It's my *job* to stimulate discussion."

"Controversial and unpleasant are two different things, as I'm sure a professional person of your intellect can appreciate."

"Look, this isn't a public service I'm fronting. It's a commercial radio station! It's my *job,* for Christ's sake! I'm good at it."

"John, please. I intend to give you every chance to prove yourself."

He was about to answer, but something in Keith's tone, a new excitement against the background panorama of bored intellect, gave him pause. "What do you mean?"

"Exactly what I say. First, tell me how you can identify whether or not a caller might have something pertinent to say?"

John frowned. "I don't know," his instinct was to be cautious, non-committal. "It's instinct I suppose. A first impression. Maybe they aren't clear on what they're saying, or don't have the ability to take the discussion anywhere useful."

"Really? On just a few simple words you can base a judgement on the intelligence and worth of the opinion *about* to be offered."

"I think so. Yes."

"John..." The warning note in Miles's voice was unnecessary. He knew he shouldn't be challenging this man, but at least while they were talking, Sandy wasn't getting hurt.

"Do you think your own opinions are worthy of national broadcast?"

"If I was bad at my job, I wouldn't be allowed to do it. You've got to see that."

"Very well John." Keith had reached a decision. It laced his words. "May I call you John? Here's what we shall do. I'm going to ask you a series of questions. I want you to answer each accurately and without hesitation. Does that sound amenable?"

John paused. "What sort of questions?" Miles was shaking his head, a frantic effort to divert him from going further. It was too late to take his advice, and they both knew it.

"Simple ones. For example, my first question is this. What is your date of birth? Well?"

What was he playing at? John hesitated, trying to grasp the point of this game. "The thirteenth of December, Nineteen Sixty-eight."

"Very well done! However you did pause ever so slightly, which might cause me to wonder if you even know your own birthday. Do you see? That would have disqualified you."

"I didn't realise we'd started."

"We haven't. The thing is, as I'm temporarily in charge of this show, I'm a little concerned that this might not be of suffic ient interest to our listeners."

John breathed a laugh. Sandy still whimpered in the background. "I don't think we have a problem there."

"Nevertheless, should you pause, or get an answer wrong, or fail to answer at all, you will be disqualified from our game. If you are disqualified, I'm going to blow Sandy's brains out."

"What? You can't..."

"Yes I can. I will do it anyway, if you refuse to submit to the test."

Miles jumped in, desperate to derail the game before it began. "Come on Keith, a normal caller doesn't have to deal with this sort of pressure."

Keith snorted. "I disagree. You obviously have no idea know how nerve-wracking an appearance on national radio can be for Joseph Ordinary. Are you ready, John?"

What could he do? Keith had him. "The questions are all that easy?"

"Every one."

John closed his eyes, wishing he had a god to pray to. "Then I'm ready."

"Excellent! When were you born John?"

He tried to switch off his worry, and focus on what he was asked. "The thirteenth of December, Nineteen Sixty-eight."

"And how old are you now?"

"Thirty-eight."

"Well done. What's your middle name, John?"

"I don't have one."

"Are you sure?"

"Of course I'm sure."

"That's a lie, John."

John went cold. What was going on? "What are you talking about? I know whether or not I have a middle name, for Christ's sake!"

"You would think so, would you not? Yet you are listed on the Radio Chat website as John T Brosnan. I'm disappointed in you, John. You lasted less time than most of the callers you cut off. Now, if you will excuse me, I'm going to go and kill my wife."

The telephone receiver clacked gently on the table, and the death sentence click of a gun being cocked filled John's dark world. His eyes were wide, the monitor burning its imprint on his retina as his breathing went shallow. He pictured the website, which he visited occasionally to answer listeners posting in the forums, and knew what had happened. "Wait! No wait! Keith! You're right! It's a mistake, I didn't give you the wrong answer! Christ, *Keith*!"

"Yes?" John was so sure it was too late that Keith's voice in his ear made him jump. "Jesus, please believe me, we're both right! I don't have a middle name! Before I worked in radio I was an actor. When you join Equity, the actor's union, you aren't allowed to have the same name as an actor already on the register. There was already a John Brosnan, so I added the 'T' to be listed separately! It doesn't stand for anything! I really don't have a middle name!"

"Is that true, Miles? Answer carefully now. If I sniff even a trace of a lie, there will be a death."

"I… I don't know. Really."

John slammed his hands on his desk. *"Miles!"*

"What he said about Equity is true, but I didn't know he was listed as John T. He's told me before that he doesn't have a middle name."

"Thank you. Well John, I'm going to do for you what I have never, in four years, heard you do for a caller. I'm going to give you a second chance."

There were tears forming in John's eyes. The studio felt tiny, and he was suddenly sure that if he stretched his arms out in any direction, he would be able to touch the walls. "Thank you. God, thank you…"

"But I warn you, my gun is now cocked. Next time there will be no hesitation. Are we clear?"

"Keith, I don't know if I can do this."

"Are you conceding my point?"

"No, I just –"

"Then when is your birthday?"

"God. December thirteenth, Nineteen Sixty-eight."

"How long have you been a radio host, John?"

"Nearly six years. Four here, two on local radio in Leeds."

"I don't like 'nearly'. So imprecise. I shall let that one pass, though. When did you lose your virginity, John?"

"My… when I was sixteen. In a caravan park."

"Was it good for you?"

"I… yes. Yes, of course it was."

"You don't sound very sure."

"Look, it was fucking brilliant, okay? Happy?"

"Content, thank you. How many brothers do you have, John?"

"None."

"And sisters?"

"Two. Both older than me."

"Ever screwed them, John?"

"No, I haven't, you sick –"

"But you've thought about it, haven't you?"

"No! Never!"

"I think the host protests too much. You never thought about it? Not even when you were young, entering puberty, with two developing women around you?"

"Keith, I…"

"Answer the question."

"I…"

"You're killing her!"

"Stop! All right! I might have done! I can't remember that far back, but I might have, all right?"

"Is the thought giving you an erection, John?"

"No."

"Miles?"

"Me neither, man."

"No, Miles. I wanted you to look and see if he has an erection or not."

"Not that I can see." Miles couldn't see anything at all, but Keith couldn't know that.

"When's your birthday John?"

"December thirteenth, Nineteen Sixty-eight, you freak."

"Freak? Me? I never wanted to fuck my sister. I left that to others." An odd thing to say, but John had no time to think about it. "Was it a ménage a trois fantasy, or would you have taken them one at a time?"

"It wasn't that detailed."

"Really? But you said you couldn't remember fantasising about them at all. Was that a lie?"

Had he said that? He couldn't remember. "No…"

"Did you lie to me, John! Did you kill my wife?"

"No! Jesus, no! *Please*!" John gritted his teeth, waiting for that deafening gunshot.

"Forgive me John. That was cruel. I won't cut you off over a trick question. What are your sisters called?"

He could barely breathe now, and his head was all over the place. "Christ." He had to pull himself together. "Carol and Anne."

"How old is Carol?"

"Forty-one."

"And Anne?"

"Forty-one. They're twins."

"Kinky. I can see why you were aroused. When were they born, John?"

"June ninth, Nineteen… Nineteen sixty-five…"

"Surely you can reel that figure off? When were the twins born, John?"

"June ninth, Nineteen sixty-five."

"What's your favourite colour?"

"Blue."

"Describe the Eiffel Tower."

"It's tall and… and pointy."

"Very eloquent. When were the twins born John?"

"June ninth, Nineteen sixty-five."

"Are you wearing headphones right now?"

"Yes."

"When were you born, John?"

"June ninth, Nineteen sixty-five."

Miles shrieked. "John!"

John heard his answer, played in slow motion in his head, and knew it was over. "No! I mean –"

"What you meant to say was the thirteenth of December, Nineteen sixty-eight, wasn't it? Are you insane, John? Don't you even know when your own birthday is?" Keith was bellowing now, all pretence at educated restraint gone. "*You don't know what you're talking about, John! I'm afraid I'm going to have to cut you off! Right now!*"

The gunshot blew John's thoughts away, as though it was he who had been shot. His head snapped back, and he was staring into Miles's shrunken pupils through the glass separating them.

Neither spoke. Neither could. Seconds thudded by, with only their ragged breathing broadcast. It was professionalism more than sense that finally forced John to speak. That dead silence, transmitted live to the nation, was almost as abhorrent as what went before. "Christ. Sweet Christ. Miles… I…"

"Oh fuck John." Miles sat, slumping away from the glass, and into the privacy of the gloom beyond.

"Do you think this is a ratings high, John? I've just made you the most famous man alive."

"You bastard."

"Careful John, you're on national radio. Besides, if you offend me I may have to kill my wife."

John blinked, all the reaction he could muster. Miles was at the window again. "What? You mean you didn't –"

"Redecorate the living room walls with her head?" Keith was nauseatingly chipper. "No Miles, I didn't. That was merely an object lesson in the pressures of live radio. John? Are you still there? You are being uncommonly quiet."

Talking required reserves of strength he could barely summon. "I'm… I'm still here."

"Then perhaps now you can –"

"Keith?" Miles sounded nervous."

"How rude. An interruption mid-eulogy. What is it Miles?"

"Just something I want to clear up, man. The police. We haven't called them, okay? When they get there, it isn't our fault." John nodded. Where was his brain? He should have thought of that.

"Oh, don't worry Miles, they're already outside. I could hardly expect to hold my tortured wife hostage on live radio without attracting their attentions. Their negotiators are most insistent. I just wanted to make sure John is crystal clear on the lessons of the past few minutes. Are you, John? Do you see now?"

"I see." He barely whispered it.

"Yes, I believe you feel it now. I'm going to go and talk to the police. Please do not try anything foolish. If your show goes off air, there will be consequences."

The familiar tap of the telephone being rested on the table, followed by receding footsteps. John stared at his monitor, trying to summon words. Even a thought would have been nice.

"John?" Miles was frightened, and John didn't blame him. "Come on man, say something."

"Say something?" He took a breath. "*Say something?* Yes, all right. Good evening ladies and gentlemen, you've tuned into the John Brosnan Murder Zone. Tonight we'll be executing one lucky lady live on air, but not before we take her apart a limb at a time. Can we also take the opportunity to point out that the views expressed on this show do not necessarily reflect the opinions of our fucking sponsors."

"John!"

"Jesus Miles, he nearly killed her! I nearly killed her!"

"Well get your bloody act together then! I can't babysit you through this!"

John was about to snap back, but stopped when he heard a clatter through the headphones. Somebody had picked up the phone. "Keith?"

"Talking to the policemen." Sandy. Her voice was flat and dull, as though she was fading away. Again, John tried to picture her, but could only come up with waxy white skin and deep circles under the eyes.

"Sandy? How are you, sweetheart? Did he bandage your hand? Sandy? Did Keith bandage your hand?"

"She's still in shock." John glared up at Miles, and motioned for him to button his lips.

"Bandaged," Sandy replied. "Bandaged it up."

"Good. That's good Sandy. That means you aren't in immediate danger, okay? We're going to make sure you're all right."

"…message…"

"What's that? What message? You want us to pass on a message?"

"For you. Message for you. From Keith. Keithy…"

"Hold on Sandy. Don't faint on us, you hear? You need to stay awake."

"…faint…"

"Come on, what's the message?" He had to keep her awake somehow. He spent his working life reaching through radios and stirring people up. Surely he could keep one fading woman awake. "You said it's from Keith. Try to concentrate. Tell us."

"Keith… best show… message… said it's the best show. Best show you've ever done."

"He…" John snapped, his forced calm burned away. "Arrogant, conceited, *fuckwit!*"

"*John!*"

"I… sorry! Keith, if you're listening, I'm sorry. I really am."

"… yours… monster…"

"What? Sandy, you're making no sense. I don't know what…"

"*Shelby!*"

There was a click, and then nothing, and for a moment John thought she had put the phone down on the table, and then he realised there was no background noise. No receding footsteps. No distant voices. Nothing.

"Sandy! Sandy! Miles, did she –"

"Hang up. Shit. Yeah."

"Keith? If you're listening to this, we haven't cut you off, understand? Sandy hung up. Just call us back, okay? Just –"

"Oh man, look at the lines…"

John did, but couldn't understand what he was seeing. They were backed up with waiting callers, from all over the country. Keith wouldn't be able to get through if he tried. "Jesus people, you're blocking the lines!" What were they doing? Did they think he was going to put them on the air *now*? "Hang up, for Christ's sake! We *will not* take your calls. Keith, if you're there, we're hanging up on everybody trying to phone in. Just keep calling. We're waiting for you to call, okay? Everybody else, *get off the fucking telephone! Right now!*"

The seconds mounted into minutes, and all John could do was shake, and watch as Miles kept hanging up on callers, answering each for long enough to find out who it was, and then letting them go.

"Got him! Line two!"

John's jaw cramped, the subconscious effort of clenching his jaw in frustration and fear taking its toll. "Keith! Keith, is that you?"

"Hello John." In the background, something snuffled. Bizarre though the image was, John pictured a pig snorting with a bad cold.

"It wasn't her fault, okay? She's in shock, she –"

"Relax, John. I'm not going to punish her for her actions."

"That's good Keith, thank you."

"I have hacked off her nose quite different reasons."

"You've…" He couldn't finish the sentence.

"Had cause to spite her face, unfortunately."

John retched as that wet background gurgle started to make sense, and swallowed his supper of bitter back coffee back down. His skin was icy. *I'm in shock too,* he thought. "God. Oh god. We didn't do anything. We... we got you back on air as soon as we could. Why?"

"Not to punish you, I can assure you of that. No, you behaved in an entirely appropriate manner, for once." Keith sniffed, a superior, horrifying sound. "I've just punished each and every caller who blocked the lines. Their need to air their sanctimonious opinions, even when someone's life is at risk, has permanently disfigured my wife."

John needed to cry, and the tears formed in his eyes, but he would not let this man hear him do so. Instead, he wrapped the grief up in appalled anger, and swallowed it down to live with the coffee. Later, when this ended, he could vomit up both. "For God's sake, listen to yourself! You can't make yourself right or wrong by hurting her!"

"You're correct of course. Violence arrests the attention, but it doesn't make the point. I'm going to move on to the culpability of others, but I'm not quite finished with the police yet."

"What... what do you want us to do while you're gone?"

"Why, the job that you proclaim yourself to be so very good at."

"I'm a talk show host! How am I supposed to do my job without a caller?"

"Take one." John couldn't believe what he was hearing. "The very first call to come through after I go. Keep them on the line, talk about me. I wish to join the discussion upon my return."

"You can't spring something like that on someone!"

"I'm hardly springing it on them John. Anybody who does not wish to be in that position should avoid calling in at all costs. I invite you to enhance my warning."

John tried. "Don't do it. Please, god. If you call in, if any of you challenge him on this, you're risking her life. Please understand –"

“It won’t do any good you know. They don’t see her. They can’t touch her. They’ll never have to meet her. There are no consequences for them. Miles?”

“All the lines are busy,” Miles murmured. “It’s jammed.”

“Take whoever’s on line one. Don’t let them go until I say so. If you cut them off or they hang up, I don’t care which, then Sandy dies.”

The receiver tapped the table, and Keith’s footsteps receded.

“Miles... I…” He sighed with resignation and grief, knowing he was trapped. They all were. Human nature, at its most ugly, guaranteed it. “Who’s on line one?”

“This is Margaret. From York.” The flattened vowels confirmed it.

“Margaret.” John felt a sudden urge to laugh, and bit down on his lip to stop from doing so. “What would you like to contribute to the… discussion, Margaret?”

“I’m…” She was nervous, and rightly so. “Well… you’ll have to excuse me, I’m a first time caller.”

“You’re a…” His control vanished, and he giggled. He knew it was hysteria, but when it got hold, it refused to let go. Beginning somewhere deep inside his fear and guilt, it spurted upwards and shook him. Tears flowed over his cheeks as he laughed out loud.

“John?” Miles sounded hysterical too, but in a different way. “John, enough!”

“She’s… she’s… a first time caller!” He could barely breathe.

“I see nothing funny in that.” Margaret sounded genuinely aggrieved. “I’m a little nervous, that’s all.”

With a mental wrench, John got hold of himself. He was sweating, despite the studio being cold. The armpits and back of his shirt were as drenched as his cheeks. “No… sorry… I can agree that live radio has its pressures. Have you been listening to the whole show?”

“I have. I’ve been listening very carefully, and I…”

Filling the gap left by his hysteria, anger surged over him. “Then Margaret, why in God’s name did you call?”

"Taking the Lord our God in vain isn't going to help you one bit."

She was one of those. She couldn't have timed it better. "Margaret, we're talking about a woman's life!"

"Our Lord has taken her fate in His hands. I called because I believe this man is attempting the Lord's work."

"What the hell are you talking about?"

Her indignation increased, as though it were John being the idiot. "He is attempting the Lord's work, but he is using the hand of Satan to accomplish it. The Lord's duty cannot be taken on by a mortal man."

"Surely that dismisses the sacrifice of His own son, a mortal man?" John had not heard Keith pick the receiver up.

"Keith…"

"I am talking to Margaret here." John swallowed his anguish. There was no way this could go well. Helplessness made him nauseous. "Haven't you just diminished Christ's own dying sacrifice?"

"Christ our Lord was no ordinary man. He was of the Three."

"Are you so certain that I am not?" There was no mockery in Keith's voice, and it drew Margaret up short.

"Pardon?"

"Perhaps I am doing the Lord's work because I am, in fact, He."

Margaret spluttered, and John imagined tea spilling from a prim little cup in her hands. "You can't… I can't… you have lost your way sir! This is blasphemy!"

"Would it be blasphemy if it came from the lips of Jesus Christ?"

"Of course not!"

"Then I say again – how do you know that I am not Christ come again? What proof can you offer?"

"Proof? *Proof?* I can offer proof from the pages of the bible!"

"This will be an education." If Sandy's life were not hanging in the balance, John might have laughed.

"Christ himself told us to turn the other cheek. Your attempt at petty vengeance discredits you!"

"Nonsense."

"The words are written!"

"Yes they are. However, they were written nearly two millennia ago. This is a new age. Perhaps the Lord would wish to change his mind."

"The Lord is constant!"

"I have to disagree there also. You quote the New Testament. The sequel. The original was better. In it, the Lord asked us to take an eye for an eye."

"It is widely accepted that… that… much of the Old Testament was metaphorical! It shouldn't be taken literally!"

"Oh, *please.* How on earth can 'an eye for an eye' be a metaphor for anything but the obvious?"

"I –"

"If you accept that God's word is represented in the Bible, then there is only one way to reconcile the obvious differences between 'an eye for an eye' and 'turn the other cheek'. At some point between testaments, God changed his mind."

"God is –"

"Fickle, apparently. Perhaps he once advised humanity that taking revenge was a wise and appropriate course of action in adversity. Later, finding that this had not worked, he revised the strategy. Further to that, perhaps he has examined the situation more recently, and decided he was right the first time. An eye for an eye."

"You… you cannot presume to know the Lord God's mind!"

"Neither can you."

"His word is written!"

"How drearily circular. Convince me that my argument is flawed. If you can't, then I shall put my own thoughts on the matter to practise and puncture my wife's eyeball."

John opened his mouth, then closed it, knowing that his interjection might just cause Keith to pre-empt his threat.

“Perhaps it will make a pop that you will be able to hear over the telephone. What do you think about that?”

“Her fate –”

“Is in the Lord’s hands? How easy for you. But the Lord gave humanity free will. Are your thoughts not your own? If that is the case then her fate lies not in His loving hands, but in yours.”

“I… the Lord… I…” It was the sound of punctured certainty.

“The eyes have it, I believe. If you will bear with me a moment, I will remove one of Sandy’s. Busy, busy.”

Sandy screamed through a face blocked with blood and phlegm.

John took a frightened breath, but Miles got there first. “Wait!”

“Yes Miles?”

“I just… I want… Keith, *why are you doing this?*”

There was a pause, pregnant with imminent violence, but then Keith spoke. “It isn’t clear?” He sounded puzzled. “I’ll spell it out then. John Brosnan has power. Enormous power, which he abuses. Yet he cannot be punished in isolation, for we must also look to the givers of power for blame. Each and every caller who rings in, certain that their opinion is the correct one, determined to make the world see that they are right, enhances the damage John can do.”

“You want to hurt John, and his entire audience?”

“They empower him. They feed him through the simple act of tuning in every evening. John devours their devotion, transforms it into malice, then sends it back to them in a feedback loop of pure vitriol. For as long as they permit it there is no hindering this perversion, but if that supply is cut off, if he is starved of sustenance, then an evil ends.”

“But –”

“Please Miles, I won’t be distracted. I owe my wife a blinding.”

Sandy snuffled in the background. “… eyes…”

“Keith, please. I’ll give you whatever you ask for. *Please*?”

"Anything? Very well, I'll give you a single chance to remedy Margaret's error."

"Name it."

It was John's turn to want to divert this before it went any further, but what else could Miles do?

Keith inhaled through his teeth, a cold hiss. "Tell me my surname."

Miles paused, his mouth open. "Oh *shit* Keith, how could I know that?"

John's eyes flew open, and something tugged his thoughts.

"By paying attention. Now, for wasting my time, I think my wife should lose both her eyes. Sandy? Hold still dear."

John's mind raced. Something had sparked at the back of his brain. Something important, to do with the timing, the point Keith was trying to make, the fact that others had fucked Keith's sister, and something Sandy had told him earlier.

"…dear…" Sandy snorted, and a clear picture of her face slammed into his mind, the snot and blood-filled wound between her eyes the only thing he could focus on.

It was enough, and he had the answer. "*Wait!*"

"My surname John," Keith snapped, "or I take both her eyes."

"Okay, you bastard." John shut his eyes, so that he wouldn't have to look at Miles if he was wrong. "Shelby. Your name is Keith Shelby."

"… monster…" Sandy knew that better than anybody.

"Oh shit, oh shit, oh shit."

"Shut up, Miles," Keith said calmly. "Congratulations John. Christie Shelby was my sister."

"Oh Christ." Miles couldn't seem to stop himself, but Keith ignored him. John was thankful.

"The people, the public, put her books on bestseller list after bestseller list. She was adored, until the murder of Rebecca McKinley. Suddenly the people believed her worse than the murderer. I would have been less aggrieved had they arrived at the conclusion independently. They did not. They knew what to think because they read it in papers, saw it on television, and heard it on the radio. You, John Brosnan, led the charge."

"Jesus Keith, John didn't want to see her dead!"

"Yet dead she is, at the hands of his church, the idiot public. They *drove* her towards the grave." Finally, there was some emotion in Keith's voice. For the first time since he had begun speaking, Keith sounded human. John tensed, because he knew how to play humans.

That meant he had a chance.

"That's enough," he said, quiet but firm. "You're wrong, Keith."

Miles shrieked like a scared girl. "John! Shut up! Just shut up!"

"Miles," Keith began, stark warning in his voice.

John cut him off. "No, it's all right Keith. Miles is right. I'm obviously not going to tell you what I think."

"You have no say in the matter. I'll –"

"Kill your wife. Yes, I know. But you'll also kill her if my argument holds water. If I'm right, she's dead. If I say nothing, she's dead. To be absolutely honest with you Keith, I'd rather you did it now." His heart was pounding at an absurd rate, but his voice held firm. He hadn't felt this way since being on stage.

"What? You can't –"

"I bloody well can. I either draw that woman's suffering out until you finally feel your point is made, or let you kill her now. I'm doing her a mercy."

His words hung in the air. Miles jumped in, as John had expected. "Don't listen to him Keith! Whatever you want, I'll do. He can't throw you off the air, not without me agreeing."

"I won't do anything else, Keith. Do you understand what I'm telling you? I don't care about your game anymore."

"I... I swear to God I'll kill her."

"*Then go ahead and kill her!* How many people will listen when they've heard you commit cold-blooded murder live on air? It doesn't matter anyway. Whatever he tells you, Miles will not allow her death to be heard over the airwaves. Why the hell would he? They'll get the build up, then nothing but jingles or dead air for the rest of the night."

"*Enough*!" Keith was actually breathing hard. John hoped he was sweating, had sensed the shift in mood and power, but when he spoke again he sounded calm. "That's enough John. I understand."

"What?" Miles sounded as tired as John felt.

"As John points out, I've applied a great deal of pressure to you both, with your only incentive to participate being the prolonged suffering of my wife. Hardly good bartering, is it? Very well. My solemn oath goes to you that if you can convince me I have erred, Sandy will not be harmed again."

"How good is your oath, Keith?" John needed to hear it.

"Oh, very good indeed. However, I cannot offer a single reassurance that you could not cast doubt upon. The decision really is yours. The first time this evening you have had that luxury. How does it feel?"

"Liberating." It was. Something in John had been set free. "I'm going to take your word for it, Keith. I'm going to show you why you're wrong."

"Oh man, be careful," Miles muttered.

"It is not advice to take lightly."

"I know that, Keith." He took a deep breath. Once he started, it would be too late to go back. It was probably too late already. "How long have you been listening to the show, Keith? You told us when you first came on, didn't you? You said you'd been listening long enough to have considered your case."

"Five years. Your entire tenure, plus the last year of your predecessor. His was a very different show, John. He listened."

"To anybody, for ages. I know. That's what killed his ratings. That's why they brought me in."

"A shock-jock is the term, I believe. An audio pornographer. A perverter of –"

"Fine," John snapped, impatience masking his nerves. He was trying to argue logic with a grief-stricken psychopath. If it didn't work… he shook the thought away, feeling Miles's eyes crawling over him. "Your complaint is with me, and those who help me spread the misery you see me spawning?"

"Yes."

"As you see it, my power comes from those who tune in to the show, who listen to what I have to say."

"Without your ratings, you would not be allowed to continue in your work."

"Another circular argument. My words have a profound effect on my listeners, but the harm could not be done if they didn't listen in the first place."

"Each one of them must be held responsible for the harm that is done not only to themselves, but also to every other individual who listens. Each is culpable in their ignorance. Ignorance is not an excuse."

"I actually agree. Look at the damage done to you and your sister, the lengths you've been driven to."

There was a sharp slap, and Sandy whimpered again.

"A reminder, lest you forget how many are affected. Sandy's pain is the direct result of the work done by you and your listeners."

John screwed his eyes closed. "Then here's what I don't get, Keith. How long have you been listening to my show?"

"As I said, five... years... wait..."

"Come on, Keith, *think*!"

"No, wait..." In a heartbeat, the surety fled Keith's voice, leaving a frightened child in its place. John couldn't stop there. Frightened children could be dangerous.

"How do you suppose you'll set an example through denial? Isn't that what you're trying to overcome? Aren't you trying to force people to see the truth? How are they supposed to do that if *you* can't?" He was growling now, trying to force the words down the microphone as though they could punch physically into Keith's head.

"*Stop it,*" Keith shrieked. "*Stop it. I swear to god I'll kill her if you don't stop talking! I'll –*"

John didn't dare to give him a moment to think. His fingernails raked his desk, but he barely noticed. "What? Break your oath? Show them the easy way out? Pretend that it's everybody else's fault, so you can continue as you are? Change their minds, Keith. Set the example. Turn off the radio. Deny me that sustenance. Come on Keith!"

"I…"

"Every second it's on, you make it worse! What are you afraid of? Turn the radio off. Turn it off, Keith. Come on, just turn it off! Diminish me! Turn the damn radio off! *Turn it off Keith!*"

"*I can't*," Keith was choked, on the verge of breaking. Which way would he go? "Don't you *understand*! I can't! Why can't I do that, John?" His voice dropped to a whisper. "Why can't I do such a simple thing?"

He had to be so careful now. "I… don't know, Keith. Habit can be crippling. But if you can't turn the radio off, then how can you expect others to? Jesus, you were going to kill your wife to make that point. Is it so much harder just to hit the off switch?"

"I… you…" Another pause, and though it was only a second, it was the longest of John's life. "You're right. You are right. Lord, I *am* wrong… do you know how painful that is? It angers me. It angers me that I am standing here, with a gun to my mutilated wife's head, being corrected by my sister's killer. You've helped me to see, and that makes me loathsome. I have done a hideous thing."

In the booth, Miles gave vent to a huge sigh. "Thank God –" John made a frantic motion, his hand slicing in front of his neck, trying to stop him. Keith needed to be wrapped in John's world, and Miles had shattered that.

"Sandy must be put out of her misery."

"What are you…" John understood. "Keith, no! You promised! You took an oath to leave her alone!"

"I'm sorry Sandy. Sorry Christie."

Sandy screamed.

The gunshot was close to the receiver, and very loud.

John was ready, and did not flinch.

He barely reacted at all.

He saw only the darkness of the studio.

There was a thud, as a body fell.

Silence followed, the appalling dead air that was the only thing capable of stirring him to speech.

"You… promised. You took an oath."

The silence did not respond.

Sandy did. "Shelby…"

"Sandy?" John sobbed the word. "Sandy, you're all right! Where's Keith, Sandy? Is he there with you?"

"Dead. Dead, dead, dead."

"Keith's dead?" Miles had found his voice again. "Oh Sandy, did you…"

"Killed himself… your monster..."

She hung up.

This time, John let the silence hang there. For once, he felt no need to fill it. He wondered if he would ever want to speak again.

"Jesus. Jesus John." Miles laughed. John knew the hysteria there well. "You did it man! Do you know what the fuck you just did?"

John stared at the monitor. He knew what he had done.

Exhaustion and grief welled in him, and he tore his headphones off.

Dropping them on the floor, he walked to the studio door.

"John? Where are you going? You can't…"

He did, opening the door and stepping out. The light of the corridor, the green carpeting stretching left and right, felt like a new world.

Behind him, Miles, twittered on. "Ah… ladies and gentlemen, we're having… uh... we're going to have to…"

John closed the door. On the tannoy in the corridor, he heard the broadcast of the show, ten seconds behind real life.

"Jesus. Jesus John. 'You did it man! Do you know what the fuck you just did? John? Where are you going? You can't...

Ah... ladies and gentlemen, we're having... uh... we're going to have to...'"

The jingle from the top of the show kicked in, as Miles tried to come up with a back up plan.

"This is a warning. You are entering the John Brosnan Zone. This is a warning. If you are of a nervous disposition, turn off your radio now. Your co-operation is appreciated. If your phone's there, you know the number. Pick up and share your wisdom with the nation. This is the John Brosnan show, and he's nothing without you."

That may or may not be true. Suddenly, John wanted to find out.

The Contributors

Andrew Humphrey

I have been knocking around the Independent Press 'scene' since the turn of the Millennium and have had stories published in magazines such as *The Third Alternative*, *Crimewave*, *Midnight Street* and *Bare Bone*. My debut collection, *Open the Box and Other Stories*, was published by Elastic Press in 2003. I have also figured in Elastic's award-winning, *The Alsiso Project* and their recent anthology, *Extended Play*. For my sins, I live and work in Norwich. My first novel, *Alison*, will appear shortly, courtesy of TTA Press. I have two sons, bless them.

"Last Kiss grew from a series of fractured, unconnected events melded with fragments of acquaintances personalities. I can't be too specific for fear of causing offence! Hopefully it all comes together ok."

Stephen Volk

Best known for creating and writing the gripping, multi award-winning ITV drama *Afterlife* starring Lesley Sharp and Andrew Lincoln, now in its second series, and the notorious, almost legendary, BBCTV "Halloween hoax" *Ghostwatch*.

An established screenwriter in Britain and the USA, his credits include *Gothic*, a retelling of the Mary Shelley/Frankenstein story directed by Ken Russell, *The Guardian*, directed by William Friedkin, and *Octane*, starring Madeleine Stowe. He won a BAFTA for his script *The Deadness of Dad* starring Rhys Ifans, and has recently written *The Interpretation of Ghosts*, for BBC Films.

His first collection of crime, horror and psychological short stories, *Dark Corners*, has been published by Gray Friar Press.

Paul Finch

A full-time writer, who works primarily in TV and film, but who is no stranger to short story markets. His first collection, *Aftershocks*, published by Ash-Tree Press in 2001, won the British Fantasy Award, while his short novel, *Cape Wrath*, made the final ballot for the Stoker awards in 2002. Other recent anthologies that he's been published in include: *Children of Cthulu, Shadows Over Baker Street, Quietly Now (A Tribute to Charles L. Grant)* and *The Mammoth Book Of Jacobean Whodunnits*. Paul has contributed regularly to *The Bill*, the popular British television crime series, while *Spirit Trap*, a teen horror movie, which he co-scripted, was released to cinemas in the late summer of 2005. Paul lives in Lancashire, northern England, with his wife, Cathy, and his children, Eleanor and Harry.

"The idea for 'Kid' first came to me many years ago, when I was still at school, though I never considered writing it as a story at the time. There were several streets in the neighbourhood where I grew up that were cul-de-sacs; they ran parallel to each other, and all terminated at the same 15-foot high wall, on the other side of which lay... well, that was the key. I had no idea what lay on the other side of it. I pondered this wall every day as I walked to school, passing one street-entrance after another, always seeing it at the far end and never knowing what it screened from my prying eyes. In truth, it was probably a scrap-merchant's yard or an office car park, but I never actually found out, despite taking measures to try and inform myself. One Saturday afternoon I wandered the entire district, seeing if I could find a way to the other side of it... and failing. I asked several adults, including two of my teachers, none of whom knew or, apparently, cared. And then, one Sunday evening at my grandparents' house, I happened to be watching a TV adaptation of one of Dickens's greatest novels, when a remarkable exchange caught my ears:

'What's on the other side of this wall?' a top-hatted chap asked a police constable.

And indeed there was a high brick wall blocking off the end of a street, just like in the neighbourhood where I grew up and went to school.

'Be glad you're on this side and not over there, sir,' the constable replied. 'Over there is the debtors' prison.'

I didn't have a clue what a debtors' prison was, but I watched the rest of the programme and was fascinated to see more: in short, it was a world where time stood still; where people who weren't criminals were confined as though they were, and yet had no limit set upon their sentence; where men and women would while away the hours, days, months, years, kicking their heels, watching the sun rise and set, gradually realising that nobody was going to come and rescue them, nobody was going to pay their debt, that they'd be there for ever because, quite simply, they'd been forgotten.

At the time it was the most profoundly disturbing concept I'd ever had to grapple with. It probably still is."

Eric Brown

Has over twenty books and eighty short stories published, and is twice winner of the BSFA award for short fiction. His recent books include the collection *Threshold Shift*, the fix-up *The Fall of Tartarus*, and the children's book *Crazy Love*. Forthcoming is the novel *Helix* (2007). He lives in Hebden Bridge with his wife and daughter. His website is at: http://ericbrownsf.port5.com/

"'The Memory of Joy' came about while thinking of an actual accident I heard of years ago, which I could never expunge from my mind. I wondered how parents might react to such tragedy, and the choices they might make if they were offered the option of having the incident wiped from their memory. By a happy coincidence I came across the line from Aeschylus quite by chance just before starting the story."

Gary Fry

Has published short fiction professionally in *Gathering The Bones* (HarperCollins/TOR), *Evernore* (Arkham House) and over 40 other publications, including the forthcoming Cemetery Dance anthology *The British Invasion*. 2006 saw the release of his first short story collection: *The Impelled and Other Head Trips* from Crowswing Books, which has an introduction from Ramsey Campbell in which the horror legend describes the author as "a master" and the collection as "an important book". Gary lives in Bradford, UK, and his favourite things in this mad world are wine, dogs and curry.

"The basic idea for my story in Choices *had been perculating for about seven years, ever since I missed a bus on my way to work. Chris's request for a tale involving a choice prompted me to develop this single notion and combine it with some thoughts I'd been developing about the nebulous nature of memory, how actual events might live on not in reflexive consciousness but in the interface between oneself and the perceptual world. The truth is on the hither side of one's subjective reality: it's not a case of peeling back the surface; it's a question of setting aside habitual, hitherto necessary interpretations of events. And a similar significent experience can bring the past tumbling back... though of course none of this precludes the choices we can make to deal with the often inevitable carnage.*

Choices are one of the major aspects of what makes us human, after all. I sincerely hope my character Louise demonstrates how choices can be used to the good, even when those around her are using them quite to the contrary..."

Richard Wright

Is an author of dark fictions living in Glasgow, Scotland. His debut novel *Cuckoo* was published in the US in 2000, and then in paperback in the UK in 2002. His short stories have appeared in anthologies and magazines on both sides of the Atlantic, and his plays *Haunter* and *Black Hearts* toured Scotland in 2001 and 2002. He has a website at www.richardwright.org where you can hunt down his fiction, download free books, or browse the inanities in his journal.

"Radio Trauma is a story now in its third incarnation. Originally conceived and written as an audio play for radio, it actually first appeared in an adapted form as the third act of my stage play Black Hearts, a linked anthology of tales for the theatre that toured Scotland in 2002. The production was remarkably true to the original concept, director Katherine Morley decided that Radio Trauma would be performed in almost total darkness, with only a single spot lit radio in the centre of the stage visible to the audience.

"When Chris Teague, editor of the book you're holding now, read the stage script of Trauma in the summer of 2006, he approached me to ask whether I'd consider turning it into a novelette, and ending his long hunt for a sixth story for Choices. Obviously, I jumped at the chance. In adapting the tale, it became clear how vast a debt I owe to Theatre Fusion, who toured the stage production, because the voices and structure the director and cast put to these characters, their beats and cadences, have hardwired into my brain, and are reflected subtly in this new version. Thanks then, to Thomas Gemmell (Keith), Donald Munro (John), Imogen Walker (Sandy), and Graeme Kerr (Miles), for bringing these characters to life. Theatre Fusion still perform new and classic theatre in Scotland, and their shows are always worth seeing."

Christopher C Teague

Born and bred in South Wales, and the editor responsible for putting together the anthologies *Nasty Snips* and *Tourniquet*

Heart, he has also written several short stories, published in print and on-line, though the output as dwindled over the last few years…

"Choices came about rather surprisingly after reading 'Not Here, Not Now' by Stephen Gallagher (Out of His Mind, PS Publishing) and it was that final sentence which struck me – the 'horror' that subtly crept up on you... I thought to myself, what a good anthology – a story about making choices ...

At first, I was going to make this an open-to-all short story collection, but I was slowly turning away from the shorter form: I found novellas and novelettes much more interesting, and therefore decided to commission six novelettes of ten thousand words each, to make a rather sizeable book of sixty thousand words. I also decided on six stories since six is the optimal number of episodes to a standard UK television drama serial – apart from the above-mentioned Gallagher tale, I was also inspired by Tales of the Unexpected and Hammer House of Horror (in the UK) along with Alfred Hitchcock Presents and The Twilight Zone (in the US).

It was those superb pieces of television that I loved whilst has a child that I wished the authors to emulate; to put together an imaginary television series to chill you late at night... who knows, perhaps some enterprising producer is reading this?

I drew up a list of prospective authors, many expressed interest, but politely declined due to time (and to be honest, I don't blame them: I may have been offering a nominal amount of money, but they had mortgages to pay...)

Thankfully, Stephen Volk said yes, then Paul Finch – Eric Brown came along when James Lovegrove mentioned in passing that he was writing something similar; Andrew Humphrey I've been wanting to publish for awhile (his collection Out of the Box is superb) and Gary Fry is an author of quiet chills to keep an eye on.

Richard Wright's place was secured by a rather chance delve into the slush-pile.

And then, I had my six. I hope you like them.

But, anyway, I wanted to turn this little biographical sketch into something more, something about the choice(s) I've made on my publishing journey; the first being a rather fateful day in 1999 when I decided to sign on that dotted line in the bank.

Then, I decided to quit a year or so later after a second book citing lack of money... but it was in my blood, and in 2002 Tourniquet Heart came out from Prime Books. It was then that I learned about digital printing, and in late 2003 I had another choice to make: to return, and publish a novella...

The Ice Maiden was published and the rest is history.

So far, there have been little choices along the way – namely deciding what to publish and what not – but nothing that will change my life, like that day in 1999.

I think that day will come between now and 2009: I'm hoping it'll mean ditching the ritual commute, but I'm wondering that by mentioning it here, I have tempted fate?

Probably.

Shit.

Anyway, I'd like to thank all six authors for providing their stories; you, the reader, for making it this far; all my customers past and present for having faith in what I've decided to publish; and also to the various book-dealers who have shown enormous faith too in buying copies off me purely on face-value – the likes of Matt of Shocklines and Andy of Cold Tonnage, to name but two, deserve utmost respect.

Coming Soon

Dalton Quayle Rides Out! by Paul Kane

Triquorum Two edited by Christopher C Teague

New Writings of the Fantastic edited by John Grant

No-Man and Other Tales by Tony Richards